CRAZY FOR THE ROCK STAR

A SWEET ROMANTIC COMEDY

ASHLEE MALLORY

ISBN: 978-0-9970035-7-4 (E-book)

ISBN: 978-0-9970035-8-1 (Paperback)

Cover design: Wicked by Design

Copy/Line Editor: Blue Otter Editing

PROLOGUE

DYLAN JAMISON—A.K.A. DYLAN CHARLES TO THE millions of fans who followed him on social media, who'd bought his last four albums, and who attended his sold-out concerts—held his hand up in a final greeting to the crowd and left the stage.

Tonight had been a great show, just as all of the shows had been on the summer tour, but with another month still left on the schedule, he was finding himself fading faster than usual. He could crash right now in his tour bus, but with at least the next hour reserved for signing autographs and greeting fans backstage, it would have to wait. Usually by this time in the tour, he'd already be itching to start writing the next songs, a few of them already taking residence in his head.

But as of now...he had nothing. His muse had seemingly left him.

Dylan had some idea why, but he refused to accept the possibility that the recent death of a man who'd run out on him and his mom before he was four would have such power over his creativity. Which was why, in the weeks

1

since he'd heard of his old man's death, he'd practiced and laughed with the band, taken his best photos with his fans, and artfully dodged questions about the end of his two-year-running love affair with a certain country music sweetheart as if there wasn't a strange emptiness inside.

His smile was brittle and his eyes glassy by the time the last fans trailed out and he said good night to the band. Getting up from his chair, he went to the cooler to grab another water, needing the hydration more than the numbing effects of the alcohol at the bar.

Behind him, the door creaked open and then quickly shut, and Dylan turned around, expecting to see someone from the stage crew telling him the coast was clear if he wanted to head out. Instead he was met with the chubby face of a girl no older than twelve, maybe thirteen, with bright red hair and brown eyes that studied him curiously.

Looked like someone slipped by the usual parade of security around the place. "Hey, kid. I think you may have taken a wrong turn somewhere."

"You're Dylan, right?"

"Uh, yeah. You're kind of young to be attending a concert by yourself," he said, easing over to the door that he pulled back open and looked out to see if there was anyone waiting. But no one was waiting, only the stage crew passing through the hallways, busy taking down and packing equipment away. He left the door open and turned back to his guest. "Are you here with your mom? Did you get separated?"

"Nope. Came here by myself. I wanted to finally meet you." She walked over to the catering table and dropped a purple backpack on the floor. "Wow. Look at all this. Do they leave all of this for you every time you have a concert?"

"Usually. Help yourself to anything you'd like."

"Really?" she asked, her eyes widening at the prospect. "Anything?"

"Sure."

She stared at the array of candy and treats, reaching out to grab something before stopping when something else caught her eye. Finally, she grabbed a couple of Red Vines and a cupcake that she took to the couch and plopped down, licking the top of a cupcake as if she hadn't a care in the world.

Unlike him. Last thing he needed was some headline alleging something untoward between him and this young girl, whoever she was. "How did you manage to make your way back here without someone stopping you?"

She shrugged. "I'm a kid. No one cares if you act like you belong. I tagged behind one of the first groups who came back here to see you. I've been waiting in the bathroom until everyone left."

Smart. And dangerous. Did she know the risks of being out alone at night in the city? "Well, I'm flattered that you took the time to come and see me, but I'm getting ready to head out. Did you have someone who's waiting to take you home?"

"Nah. I took the bus out and then took an Uber here."

"A bus? From where?"

"Santa Rosa."

"Santa Rosa?" He looked at his watch. Nearly midnight. That was almost a seven-hour trip. "And how are you getting back?"

She ignored the question. "Why did you change your name? To Dylan Charles?"

He blinked. That was pretty random. "Privacy, I guess. Look, I've got to say, kid, I'm kind of worried about you. Do your parents know you're here?"

"I left my mom a note, but she's working a double tonight, so she probably won't find out until she gets home."

This was worse than he thought.

"Mr. Charles? You're all set," a burly security guy said from the door.

Dylan whipped around, desperate for someone to get him out of this fiasco. "Great. Actually, could you do me a favor and find the stage manager?" he asked, and nodded his head toward the girl. "Looks like we have a straggler who's going to need some assistance with getting home."

"Please," she said, rolling her eyes. "I got here okay, didn't I? Besides, I'm not ready to go until you and I talk. That's why I'm here."

The security guy caught his eye and nodded, giving Dylan a sense of relief to know he was heading out to find someone—anyone—who could take control of the situation other than him.

"Okay," he said when the guy left. "What is so important that you came all the way out here to see me?"

Her bravado seemed to fail her for a moment as she glanced down at her fingernails. "When I saw you were playing in LA, I figured it was my chance. So I saved up my money and bought the bus ticket."

"The chance to what?"

She bit into her licorice, taking her time as she chewed. "The chance to meet my brother."

Her brother? The kid was crazy. "Sorry, kid. I think you must be mistaking me for someone else. Charles isn't my real last name, it's just—"

"The name you chose. I know. Just like I know your real last name is Jamison. Like mine."

That stopped him in his tracks. How did she...

"I'm Elle Jamison. My dad's name is Brick Jamison. Just

4

like yours. You probably heard that he died last month and I figured you might want to meet me since we have so much in common, what with both of us losing the same dad."

Brick Jamison. It was strange hearing that name out loud even though it was playing in the back of his own mind since he'd heard the news of Brick's death. But it wasn't something welcome, never had been since Brick had walked out on him and his mom. It was why Dylan had changed his own when he hit the road, not wanting any association with the old man.

"Sorry, kid. But the name Brick Jamison doesn't mean anything to me. Now, I think we need to get ahold of your mom and let her know where you are. Then I'm going to have someone from the crew drive you home."

"No. You're wrong. I can prove it." She dug into her pocket and pulled out a rumpled photo that she held out to him.

Reluctantly, he took it and steeled himself for whatever he was about to see. The image was of a man very much like the one featured in his mom's old photos—at least before she'd burned most of them—only now his face was more weathered and weary. On his lap was a young girl about eight with bright red hair and a toothy smile who, not surprisingly, looked a lot like his young guest. It was like a kick in the gut to see Brick Jamison, and he'd be lying if part of it wasn't a twinge of jealousy. After ducking out on Dylan, looked like Brick had decided to stick around for this one. Well, good for Elle. But it didn't improve his opinion of the old man.

He handed the photo back. "Look, whatever you think was going to happen here isn't going to happen," he said, his tone terse. "I didn't know my old man and I have no interest in knowing anything about him now. I'm sorry that you came all the way here, but there's nothing more we have to say."

There was a rapping on the door and he looked over to find the stage manager standing there. "Sorry about this, Dylan. I don't know how she got by security. But we can take care of things from here if you want to head out."

"Wait." She looked so devastated, her brown eyes brimming with tears, her head shaking side to side. "You really are my brother. Don't you want to go get some dinner or something? You can hear about me and my mom."

"I'm sorry, Elle. It's not going to happen. But what I am going to do is make sure you get home safe and sound."

She jumped to her feet, her chin trembling. "You're just a dumb jerk, and I can't believe that I spent my entire savings coming here to see you."

"Sorry to disappoint you. If Brick Jamison is your father, then I'm sure it's something you're used to. Take care, Elle." He took one last look at her now tearful face, her eyes already narrowed with anger, and turned away.

He was a dumb jerk. He could own that. But he was also bone-weary tired and admittedly shaken by having a ghost from his past confront him in the form of a young girl who had no idea of the kind of risks she'd taken upon herself coming here tonight.

He needed sleep. That's all. Some rest and recuperation.

Then, in the morning, he'd be ready to process the bomb she'd just dropped on him.

ONE

THE SUN HAD DROPPED BELOW THE ROLLING HILLS OF the Sonoma Valley hours before, leaving only the trickle of moonlight above and the beams from Tessa's car to guide her down the familiar bumpy road that, in her aging jalopy of a car, threatened the car's entire structure with every bounce and dip.

Up ahead, she could make out the outline of her family's farmhouse, the front porch lights flipped on even though everyone who still called the place home was back at the hospital. It made the place seem eerily quiet, particularly for a Tuesday in October, one of the busiest months of the year for the harvest. But as her brother had assured her, the Chardonnay and Pinot Noir grapes had already been harvested, and the Cabernet could still be weeks from their peak, leaving only the Montenegro farm's apples for harvesting.

Tessa parked the car and sat for a moment as tears of terror and relief slipped down her face. She'd kept them at bay since the moment she first received her brother's call saying that their dad had been in an accident while working on the farm and had been rushed to the hospital, keeping her cool as she threw some things together and drove from San Francisco to the hospital in Sonoma. She'd stayed calm and level-headed as she greeted her brothers, met the doctor and nurses, and then delicately hugged her dad, who, although bruised and sore and scheduled for hip surgery in the morning, was in relatively good spirits. It was only now, safe under the shadow of her childhood home, that she gave in to the emotions that had been tearing at her.

At least he was going to be okay. A bit banged up, but with rest and time to heal, he'd survive. She hadn't lost him.

Wiping her tears away, Tessa Montenegro took a deep, restoring breath before grabbing her bag off the seat and getting out of the car. She made her way to the back entrance to the house, taking a moment to breathe in the sweet aroma of apples that lingered in the chilly air. Someone had left the light on over the large kitchen island, basking the room in a soft light, and she looked around the room that held some of her best memories. Tessa's mom showing her how to roll the dough for the Christmas sugar cookies as Tessa slipped bites of the sweet dough into her mouth. Tessa making her first batch of cinnamon rolls with dubious success even as her brothers scarfed them all down with no complaints. The entire family gathering around the large farmhouse table to celebrate every birthday, Thanksgiving dinner, and Christmas breakfast. This place centered her. It didn't just represent her childhood. It represented everything that made life worth living. Love. Happiness. Laughter. Family.

Heading to the stove, Tessa picked up the kettle and filled it with water before placing it on the burner to boil. Grabbing her suitcase again, she headed to her room, needing to get into something more comfortable than the skirt and heels she'd put on when she first headed to work this morning. She'd been reviewing pages of real estate contracts for a large project she was assigned to when her brother Finn had reached her. She'd barely had time to stop at home to throw some clothes into a bag before getting on the road to reach her dad.

The floorboards creaked under her steps in the usual pattern as she headed upstairs and down the hallway to her room. Flipping on the light, she kicked off her shoes and tossed her bag on the bed before unbuttoning her shirt and tossing it on the back of the chair where she'd spent hours upon hours reading growing up. Her skirt came next, tossed on top of the shirt since she was too weary to bother with hanging either of them. She was digging out her yoga pants and favorite tee shirt when a creak from the hallway stopped her.

She paused and listened, half convinced she'd made up the sound since this was Blossom Falls. Nothing remotely criminal ever happened here. But, sure enough, the creaking was persistent as it reached her bedroom door.

Tessa scanned the dark room, trying to figure out her next move. Her trophy for Best in Sportsmanship from summer camp when she was twelve could be a weapon if she thwacked someone hard enough. Or maybe she should just throw herself under the bed and wait the prowler out? But surely he or she already knew she was home...

She was still standing there trying to decide when a very solid, very manly form filled the doorframe, and she couldn't stop the yelp that ripped from her throat, even as she tried to process what she was seeing. Or rather, who she was seeing. Because the person standing in front of her was the last person she'd expected to see darkening the door-frame of her bedroom ever again.

Dylan Jamison. Who, from the easy grin that broke across that still-too-handsome face, wasn't as surprised to see her as she was him. Her heart lurched in her chest, an unfair reaction considering the fear he'd put in her moments before.

"Why, Tessa Montenegro. Aren't you a sight for sore eyes," he drawled in that lazy southern accent that he only pulled out when he was trying to sweet-talk some girl into something she knew better than to consider. An accent he'd picked up having spent the first twelve years of his life living somewhere south of Birmingham, Alabama, before coming to live with his aunt here in Blossom Falls, a sleepy little farming town in Sonoma, California. His gaze dropped and that grin of his grew even wider.

Holy Josephine.

Her own eyes widened as she remembered her current state of undress and she whipped her hands up in a valiant attempt to cover herself. She frantically searched the room for something to put between herself and those brown eyes that sparkled with a little more than friendly familiarity. She spotted her quilt folded neatly on the edge of the bed and attempted to whirl it around herself. Unfortunately, it took her three tries to successfully bring it around her, leaving her all too aware of his unflinching stare and too-amused smile.

"What on earth are you even doing here?" she asked.

He leaned against the doorjamb and crossed his arms over his chest, making it impossible for her to miss the biceps straining against the sleeves of his shirt. Dang. Her guess that his appearance on the cover of his last album had been heavily airbrushed had obviously been wrong. "I had some downtime and Finn invited me to stay for a while. I take it no one mentioned this to you before?"

She was going to kill her brother. How could he go and invite Dylan Jamison to stay here without even telling her? Of course, Finn would have no idea of the feelings she'd once held toward his best friend, or of the one and only kiss they'd shared that had eclipsed anything she could have ever hoped for—just before he left her without a word to seek whatever fame and fortune awaited him.

And why did he have to have that smug smile on his face, as if he could still see her through the fabric of the quilt even though she was almost certain he could not. She lifted her chin a notch, hoping she sounded less vulnerable and shaken than she felt. "No. My brother most definitely did not mention you. How long are you staying? The weekend?"

"A little longer than that. We're working together on a business proposition."

"A business proposition? With Finn?"

A loud, shrilling whistle from downstairs reminded her that she had put the kettle on. Her initial impulse was to race down the stairs to stop the piercing sound, but the fact she was still undressed under the blanket kept her frozen in place.

Dylan seemed to be aware of the same thing as his eyes glimmered dangerously at her. "You want to go get that?

Instead of responding, she kept her eyes steady on his as the whistling grew more piercing. She'd grown up with five rough-and-tumble brothers who could easily out-race and out-tackle her if they'd wanted to during a squabble. Which was why she'd perfected the subtle art of staring. She could stare the best of them down into complying with her wishes.

Ten seconds.

What? Had he gotten too cheap to pick up a razor in the past week?

Twenty seconds.

He certainly hadn't gotten too cheap to let go of his gym membership if the hard, rippled muscles outlined in that tee shirt were any indication.

Thirty seconds.

"Fine," Dylan said, and sighed. "I'll get it. See you downstairs."

He stepped back, keeping eye contact with her until he reached the hall, finally turning away. Tessa rested her hand over her heart to try and stop the annoying hammering.

Ten years. It had been ten years since Dylan Jamison crushed her when he walked away from her and everything she tried to offer him. She'd been devastated at the time, especially on the heels of her mom's death, and she'd barely made it out of the dark, sucking depression that had clouded her world at the time. She'd vowed to leave all her childish dreams and fantasies behind her from that moment on.

When she reached the university where she'd once envisioned majoring in art a month later, she switched gears completely and turned her eyes on something more practical and sustaining—law. After all, she'd been pretty good at it when she'd worked part-time at Jasper's law office during high school, moving up from simple filing and receptionist duties to actually helping him draft motions and various contracts.

It hadn't been easy over the years, putting Dylan Jamison out of her mind and her heart, especially after his first album went platinum and his face started appearing on the pages of the popular magazines that lined the expressway of her local supermarket or those unpredictable moments when his voice could catch her unaware sitting in traffic playing across the airwaves of her car radio.

She supposed it was inevitable that they'd come face-to-face again. He was still friends with Finn and the rest of her brothers, and his aunt Daphne helped oversee the operation of the family farm. Fortunately, his busy touring schedule prevented him from getting home very often over the years, and with school and then work as her usual escape, she'd been able to time her visits to avoid him. But their inevitable meeting again was supposed to be on her terms. It wasn't supposed to occur when she was feeling so emotionally vulnerable and especially not when she was standing practically naked in front of him.

It's only for the night. One night, Tessa. You got this.

After tonight, she could go on pretending Dylan Jamison didn't exist.

She dropped the blanket and dug more furiously through the suitcase until she found what she needed and pulled the clothes on.

He was not going to dictate her emotions again. She would not let him. She was in control of her emotions.

And if all else failed, she could pretend with the best of them.

———

DYLAN GRABBED the kettle from the burner and the shrill whistling decreased to a loud hiss, giving him an opportunity to organize his thoughts.

He'd known that accepting Finn's invitation to come to the farm for a few weeks could potentially bring him face-to-face with the youngest of the Montenegro brood. But the offer of solace and a possible business prospect to distract him from his personal woes had been too tempting to resist. He'd been on his way back from LA after meeting with his agent when his aunt texted him about Joe Montenegro's accident earlier. She assured him that Joe would be fine but would need hip surgery in the morning, so Dylan decided not to foist himself on Tessa and had returned to the farm.

He'd heard her come up the stairs and head past his room, her quiet footsteps unmistakable compared to the sturdier footfalls of her brothers, and he had debated whether or not to give her some space and wait until morning to say hello. But his curiosity had gotten the better of him, and he'd slipped down the hall, telling himself his interest was more in finding out firsthand the health of Joe Montenegro and less about seeing Tessa after all these years.

In all the years he'd known Tessa, he had treated her like Finn's sometimes pesky, sometimes endearing, headstrong younger sister, one he could tease and cajole mercilessly. For the most part. At least until that fateful Christmas he'd returned home from college and had been stunned to see the youngest Montenegro had grown up and become a beautiful, headstrong young woman who made him think of things that would have been shocking before. He'd been sure to stay clear of her ever since, up until that day he heard word that Tessa's mom had died and he returned home to pay his respects. For two weeks, they'd reached a new level of their friendship, one where he stopped treating her like Finn's younger sister and treated her like a friend. A friend who he'd tried not to think about kissing.

So when they'd had that one moment out by the pond, a moment he cursed himself for later as his taking advantage of a vulnerable young girl, one who he could never have a future with for obvious reasons, he'd realized he was in dangerous territory and he needed to get away immediately for both their sakes.

He hadn't seen her since.

A flash of smooth white skin, a thin waist curving to full hips covered in polka dot panties, and a lacy bra with pink bows filled his brain and he stopped.

So maybe trying to scare the crap out of her hadn't gone exactly as he'd planned.

He remembered the cold fury that filled her pretty green eyes as her face flushed red. It was clear she hadn't forgotten his abandonment all those years before, something he couldn't fault her for. But he'd done what he had to do to make sure that she got over him and moved on, that she didn't hold on to some childish crush that would keep her from reaching everything she was meant to achieve in her life. He wouldn't be the reason for holding anyone back. He wasn't like his old man. And from all accounts, he'd been right to do what he had. Tessa had gone on to be a success, working at some fancy law firm in the city and definitely heading up in the world.

A rustling behind him told him that she'd arrived, and he turned to see her cross the kitchen floor in loose-fitting yoga pants and an oversized white tee shirt that hung past her hips. No doubt an attempt at hiding any glimpse of the soft curves he'd caught before, something he thought with both disappointment and relief.

The silence stretched out awkwardly, and he found himself needing to fill it, to get back somehow to their former friendship. "So how's your dad doing? I was going to stop by earlier, but I figured there'd be enough comings and goings I didn't need to add one more body to the mix."

"The hip will need surgery first thing in the morning, and he sprained his wrist when he caught himself, but overall he's in good shape," Tessa said and headed to the cabinet, where she pushed things aside until she found a familiar blue mug that she set on the counter and dropped a tea bag into. "The recuperation is going to be the killer, since once he's released from the hospital, he's going to be completely reliant on everyone else to help him. Aidan and Liam have already offered to chip in to help cover the cost of a home care nurse above what his insurance would provide, so that's a huge relief," she said, referencing two of the five Montenegro brothers who lived out of state and couldn't make it home.

"He's definitely going to hate that."

She walked over to the other side of the island and slid onto a barstool. "Undoubtedly."

She'd cut her hair, he realized, watching as she tried to tuck a strand of it behind her ear only to have it spring back into place. Instead of thick waves that fell down her back, it now barely brushed the bottom of her jawline, making her appear more gamine, more mischievous, but just as pretty. After another attempt to tuck the hair away, she blew it from her face, satisfied when it seemed to stay away even if temporarily. "You mentioned something about a business proposition with Finn? What's that about?"

He looked away, needing to keep his focus. "Well, you know how traditional the guy is, always has been. He hated when he was outvoted a few years ago and half the orchards were torn out to make way for the grapevines."

She nodded. "We all hated to do it, but with Aidan and Liam both gone and Finn in school, Dad needed to cut expenses and bring in more income. And grapes have become the highest-yielding cash crop in recent years."

"Which is why he's been so determined to find a way to make the orchards just as viable. I think he's onto something." He grabbed a brown, unmarked bottle from the fridge and set it down in front of her. "Look familiar?"

"I'm guessing it's a bottle of our cider."

He nodded. Ever since Dylan could remember, the Montenegros had brewed small batches of hard cider from the harvested apples. It had been a tradition since Emilio Montenegro, Tessa's grandfather, had first arrived in California from Portugal and bought the farm and the orchards for his own family. Of course, Dylan and Finn weren't legally old enough to sample the stuff at most of the Thanksgivings, but they'd still managed to sneak in a few sips when they thought no one was looking.

"Finn's gotten it in his head that with the resurgence of hard cider of late, why shouldn't Montenegro Farms take a shot at making it marketable?" He grabbed a couple of glasses and poured them each a small amount. "He's been tinkering around with a few recipes and a couple months ago pulled me into it."

"But why would this involve you?" she asked, lifting the glass and taking a sniff. Her fingernails, he noted, were still chewed down to the quick, a habit that it looked like she hadn't been able to break, which for some reason reassured him that some things did remain the same. "You're not a farmer. You probably don't even know the difference between a Gravenstein and a Cortland."

"Probably not, but if he's going to make a real go of this, he needs an infusion of cash to buy the equipment, the supplies, and the manpower the business is going to need. In short, he needs an investor."

"Surely you don't have to be here for that. Can't you just write a check?"

"Sure. I could. But that's not what this is about. It's a partnership. I'm going to give him not just my money but my name recognition." Tessa didn't need to know that, right now, Dylan desperately needed something to distract himself with, and getting this business off the ground was going to provide that. But it was more than just that. He believed in this product and his friend, and he wanted to do whatever he could to help make this venture a success. "Rocking Blues Cider. That's the name of our new venture if you're curious. Go ahead. Try it," he said and nodded to her glass.

Cautiously, she took a sip. "Pretty good. It's familiar, but also different than the usual harvest cider." She took another taste. "All right, so it sounds like an interesting business venture. But why do you have to be *here*? Can't you consult and write checks from LA?"

"Let's just say that I needed a little downtime from my life. A break, even temporary." There was also the added benefit that Blossom Falls was only a twenty-minute drive from Santa Rosa, the city where Elle Jamison lived with her mom. But that was more information than he was about to go into right now, at least until he heard back on the blood tests that would confirm the truth of Elle's paternity.

"Does this have something to do with recent rumors that you and Roxie Mann have split?" she asked him slyly.

He studied her curiously, wondering just how much of his life she'd followed over the years. The good and bad. "You know, you shouldn't believe half of what's printed about me."

She looked appalled. "Please. I don't read any of it. It just so happens that my roommates, Anna and Quinn, are huge fans, and after you made an appearance at Anna's sister's wedding this summer, she's been more obsessed. She must have mentioned the breakup."

"Sure," he teased, making it clear he didn't believe her.

"Good to see some things haven't changed over the years," she said, rolling her eyes even if the flood of pink in her cheeks told a different story. "Still as full of yourself as ever. How do you walk and not trip over that ego of yours?"

"Lots of practice."

Her lips twitched and he was certain she was fighting back a smile as her green eyes sparkled back at him. She'd always had a great smile, and it struck him how much he wanted to see it now. See she was happy.

"How does my dad feel about this business venture?" she asked, fortunately unaware of his thoughts.

"He's as excited as Finn to see the orchards become viable again." He turned and put the cider back in the fridge.

"Well, good for Finn. I hope this all turns out. Now"— she slipped off the barstool—"I think I'm going to head to bed. I want to get to the hospital early enough to see Dad off before surgery."

"Tessa," he said, waiting until she met his gaze again. "If my being here makes you uncomfortable, I can always find somewhere else to stay. I know that what happened the last time I saw you—"

"Please. Don't worry yourself about that. It was just a kiss. It meant nothing."

Ouch. It sure as hell had meant something to him, which was why he'd realized even then he had to get away. But he wasn't about to admit that, especially in light of her stated feelings on the subject. "Okay. I'm glad to hear that," he lied. "But I can find somewhere else to stay all the same."

"Like I said, I'm over it all. You're free to stay as long as you need." She picked up her dishes and took them to the sink. "Besides, if everything goes according to schedule tomorrow, I'll be back in the city by dinner."

He nodded, wanting to say something about how her

family would love it if she stuck around a little longer, but realizing it wasn't his place.

"Good night, Dylan. And if I don't see you before I leave, I wish you and Finn luck on this new venture," she said ever so politely, like they were bare acquaintances saying farewell. Not like someone who, once upon a time, had kissed him with such hope and promise that he'd been questioning his entire future without her in it.

He listened to Tessa make her way up the stairs and to her room, the sound of her shutting door echoing in the silence of the house.

And to think he'd been worried about this confrontation all this time, and for what? She was obviously completely and totally over him.

Which was a good thing, right?

TWO

Tessa stared at her dad lying in his hospital bed the next morning, studying him as he slept just as she had since they first rolled him out from surgery. She and three of her five brothers, Finn, Declan, and Rowan, had all taken turns sitting with him through most of the morning, anxious to see him awake and feeling better, before Rowan had to take off for his classes at the culinary institute and Finn and Declan headed home to shower and change.

Restless, she got up to rearrange the small bouquet of flowers she'd snipped from her mom's flower garden. Tessa knew that the flowers her mom had once proudly pruned and tended were long gone and the flowers before her had been planted and cared for by Dylan's aunt Daphne as her own gesture toward the memory of her best friend, something Tessa was grateful for.

She sat down again, willing herself to close her eyes for a few minutes since God knew she hadn't gotten much sleep last night, not with Dylan Jamison just down the hall from her. To say it had been a shock to see him standing across from her after all these years was an understatement. She'd been relieved that she'd managed to form sentences and hadn't resorted to name-calling or throwing things at his head as she'd imagined doing over the years. She had to congratulate herself in staying calm and level-headed and appearing completely unaffected by his visit, even if inside she'd felt anything but.

She closed her eyes against the old pain of loss and disappointment when she thought about Dylan and how he'd disappeared from her life as quickly as he'd reappeared then, just as now.

The difference was that she was no longer a lovelorn, naive young girl who still clung to the possibility that one day he would wake up and see she wasn't just his best friend's little sister, but a young woman who had been in love with him since he first appeared at the farm as an angry, sullen twelve-year-old boy. Back then he'd just lost his mom to the ravages of drugs and wasn't willing to accept that he could have a clean start in Blossom Falls with a loving aunt who would care for and nurture him, as well as a close-knit community who would watch out for him as they had for all of them. How could she not fall in love with the kid who'd pretended he didn't need anyone? It was part of Tessa's DNA to want to fix things.

But over time, it had evolved into more than puppy love, and she'd waited, hoping for something more. Even that dark day her mom died and Dylan had arrived home again to pay his respects, she still had hope. She hadn't had any expectations when he walked into that church and took his place in a pew next to his aunt, meeting her gaze for the barest of seconds and taking a little of her pain away in that moment. She certainly hadn't thought he would stick around one week, let alone two weeks, cheering her up by trying to cook for her, playing games and making jokes, and taking long walks around the farm. He'd been the one who forced her to go back to the art studio, where she'd turned to the only medium she knew where she could put all her pain and create something positive.

It was on that last night, sitting under the stars on the old jumping rock out by the pond, that he'd finally kissed her. And for a moment, she saw a future filled with something other than the sadness that had overtaken her. But the hope had been brief when, the next morning, before she'd even stirred from bed, Dylan had left. Gone back on the road with his band to try and get his name out there. And he had been successful, even if he'd crushed her heart in the process. A week later, she'd tucked away all her foolish childhood dreams, including her art and a future with Dylan Jamison.

From the bed, there was a slight rustling, and she glanced over to see her dad's hand moving, then his eyes opening. "Hi, Daddy," Tessa said and went over to stand at his side.

"Hey, pumpkin," he said, his words spoken with half the strength he usually projected. "Sorry I gave you all such a scare yesterday. Taking you away from your work."

"You didn't take me away from anything. Nothing is more important than your health." She studied him. He appeared tired, his eyes heavy and his still-handsome face drawn downward, weighed down by pain and drugs. But other than a bruise on his forehead, a few scratches on his cheek, and his arm resting in a sling, he seemed to be okay. "How are you feeling? Are you in pain?"

"Not too bad, all things considered. I'll be doing a lot better once I get out of this place and into my own bed."

She nodded, not exactly sure if that was going to be as

soon as he thought. The doctor who performed his surgery had told them it was going to be a slow healing process that would include daily exercise with the help of a therapist and a lot of bed rest. "Are you sure you're going to be okay with me heading back to the city? I could stay a few more days, be home with you when you get out of the hospital. I don't mind," she tried again even though he'd been clear last night and this morning right before surgery that she should get back to the city as he'd be just fine.

"But I would mind," he countered. "You didn't work so hard over the years to get where you are only to risk everything to play nursemaid for me. That's why your brothers are getting me that home nurse to babysit me."

She laughed. "A home nurse can hardly be called a babysitter, and it beats having to go to a care facility, doesn't it? You know that with your limited mobility, it's going to be an effort to get in and out of bed for a few days, which means you're going to need someone to be there to take care of you—wanted or not. Just until you're a little further along."

He snorted. "A babysitter. Like I said."

She did not envy the people who were going to be in earshot of her dad for the next week. He hated relying on other people. Poor Dylan.

That thought cheered her up immensely.

"Glad to see you're awake, Dad," Finn said, appearing in the doorway with two coffees. "I thought you might need a little wake me up from some decent coffee," he said and handed a cup to Tessa along with three sugars.

"I told you to go on home and get some rest," their dad said.

"I did. Long enough to catch some sleep, shower, and

give the crew some direction for the day. My only priority now is to make sure you're okay."

Tessa ripped the sugar open and poured it in. She knew she could certainly use this considering she hadn't slept the night before, waking in the early hours, determined to avoid seeing Dylan again. Speaking of which... "So, Finn. I had a bit of a scare last night, coming home to what I thought was an empty house. Did you guys forget to mention our new guest?"

"Oh, hell. That's right," Finn said, taking a drink of his coffee. "It completely slipped my mind you didn't know Dylan was bunking with us."

"How long exactly is he sticking around?" she asked, blowing on the top of her coffee, trying to sound casual.

"Not sure exactly. You don't mind, do you?" he asked, looking puzzled.

"Of course not. I just would have appreciated a little heads-up, is all. I hear you guys are going into business together as well?"

"Still can't believe it myself, but yes we are. Figure if the boys over in Sutter Falls can make a go of it with that weak-assed shi—crap," he corrected as he glanced at his dad, "then why can't we? I have a lot more experience on the subject and hands down the best apples to work with on the West Coast."

For the next few minutes, her dad and Finn discussed the potential diseases they might find in some of the older sections of the orchard while Tessa studied them. It was good to see Finn looking so excited about something again. Of all the siblings, he seemed to have taken on the most responsibilities on the farm, working side by side with her dad and assuming the burden of figuring out how to keep the farm viable, all while he also attended the university, attaining his horticultural degree.

Declan and Rowan were around, too, of course, but with Declan often working consecutive days and nights at the firehouse and Rowan's days at the culinary school followed by long shifts working at the bottom of the totem pole at one of the high-end restaurants over in Napa, the place was practically empty. And with Aidan in Seattle working some IT tech job, and Liam, returning two years ago from his last tour in Afghanistan, doing top-secret security work around the country, Finn and their Dad were the only regular occupants in the large, rambling farmhouse. Leaving everything on Finn, which was why seeing his face light up with excitement at a project of his own was rewarding in itself.

Even if it did bring Dylan Jamison back into their lives.

The conversation was interrupted by a knock at the door, and Daphne Jamison peeked her head in, her concern etched in the lines of her face. "Hello. I hope I'm not interrupting anything..." Daphne said, and slowly eased into the room.

"Of course not," her dad said from the bed. "Come on in. The more the merrier."

Daphne had become as much a part of the Montenegro family as her nephew had over the years. Hired as a farm hand and working her way up to a management position, she'd become indispensable. When Tessa's mom had died, they knew that in those initial months while her dad processed his grief, the farm would be safe in her capable hands. Over ten years since then, Tessa had witnessed a sort of friendship evolve between Daphne and her dad, something that had given her a sense of relief in knowing he had someone to rely on. Sometimes Tessa got inklings that

Daphne's feelings might have grown past pure platonic emotions, but her dad would never be able to return those feelings having lost the love of his life in his wife. He'd said as much himself multiple times over the years.

"Well, you definitely seem to have improved since yesterday," Daphne said and walked over to the vase of flowers Tessa had brought. She was still wearing her work overalls. Her blond hair, woven in gold just like her nephew's, was pulled back into a simple and practical bun. "These are lovely. From your mom's garden?"

Tessa nodded. "Although I think it's probably more yours now. You've done such a great job with it over the years." Tessa would have hated to see the garden turn to weeds.

"Thanks, sweetie. And how are you doing? I'm afraid things were so stressful yesterday I didn't really get a chance to catch up. You enjoying your job?"

Enjoying? That was maybe a stretch. "It definitely keeps me busy," she said instead. "I saw Dylan at the house last night. I hadn't realized he was staying in town. That must be nice for you, after having him away for so long."

"Absolutely. If I hadn't transitioned his old room into my workshop, I'd have loved to have him stay with me. Fortunately, your dad and brothers were generous enough to put him up at the house."

"The boy is always welcome. He's family, just like you," her dad said fondly.

"Looks like I made it in time for the party," Declan said from the doorway. He was a little shorter than Finn— not that she needed to remind him of that—but just as handsome with the same strong features, same rich dark brown hair, but with green eyes like hers instead of Finn's blue.

"I'm glad you made it, as I was just getting ready to head out," Tessa said.

"What's the rush?" Finn asked. "It's Wednesday. Might as well just call it a week and hang out with your old bros. With Dylan in town, it will be just like old times. You pestering us while we completely ignore you."

Sad but true. "As tempting as that sounds, I actually do have to get back this afternoon. I'm sure I already have a mountain of work waiting for me as it is. You guys will have to keep me updated if anything changes. I'm curious to see how having this home nurse works out."

"Oh, I'm sure disastrous. You know Dad."

"I'm still here. Still awake," her dad said from the bed. "And as long as he or she respects my boundaries, there won't be a problem."

They all looked at each other, biting back their laughter.

"I'm sure it will all be just fine," Daphne jumped in. "Don't worry about anything."

Daphne's phone chirped and she glanced down. "Looks like Dylan's on his way. Did you need him to bring anything from the house?"

While they consulted, Tessa came to her feet, not needing any more reason to get out of here than another run-in with Dylan Jamison. "I guess I probably should get on the road," she said, going over to kiss her dad's cheek. "If you need me, you'll call, right?"

"Sure, honey. But I'll be fine. I'm sure with this brood and my new babysitter, I'll be in good hands."

That was about as good as she could ask for, she supposed. With a final good-bye, she left the room, relieved to make her escape before Dylan arrived, even if a little sad to leave the cozy room filled with her family.

But that was what growing up was all about, wasn't it?

Moving on? Getting out into the world to try new things, have adventures and experiences that you wouldn't have if you stayed home?

Once upon a time, the thought of staying in Blossom Falls had felt suffocating and boring. Especially after the day that Dylan Jamison had picked up and left, giving her all the more reason to want to move on, too.

Ironically enough, now he was back. And she was the one leaving.

"I'M REALLY sorry about all this, Eric. I hope you can understand that, right now, with things so busy at work, I just don't really have the time to have a go at a relationship, which is totally unfair to you," Tessa explained to her date on Saturday night as they sat in his car outside her place.

It was their fourth date, and she was pretty certain that he had been expecting a lot more than the brush-off tonight. But after the scare with her dad and the run-in with Dylan that left her feeling scared and vulnerable all over again, it reminded her of all the reasons why dating was a bad idea right now.

Eric's face dropped in disappointment as he sat there, unsure what to say, and she felt a pang of guilt. He was good-looking, kind, and had a steady job, all things that deserved a check in the must-have column.

"You're really a great guy, though, and I know some lucky woman will snatch you up in no time."

He met her gaze, confusion in his eyes. "This comes as a bit of a surprise, I'll admit. I thought we were hitting it off pretty well. But I guess if that's how you feel..."

Her hand was on the handle of the door and she pulled it, ready to get this part over. "I think so."

"Maybe we could still grab a coffee sometime?" he asked, his tone hopeful.

"Maybe." She got out and paused before shutting the door. "Take care, Eric."

"You, too, Tessa."

Without wasting any more time, Tessa shut the door and ran up the steps to the three-bedroom duplex she called home. After unlocking the door, she stepped inside and felt a wave of relief that she'd gotten through tonight.

"Hey. You're home pretty early for a Saturday," her roommate Quinn said, glancing up from her computer, tucking a strand of brown hair behind an ear.

"What about you?" Tessa asked, dropping her keys and purse on the small hall table. "I thought you and James were heading to Idaho to talk wedding plans with your mom?"

"That was the plan, but James got called away to Chicago last minute and won't be back until tomorrow."

"Tessa, good timing," her other roommate, Anna, said, coming from the kitchen carrying her laptop, her blond hair pulled into a high ponytail. "I need your opinion on this story I've been working on. Can you read it for me?"

A full house then, unusual of late, especially for a Saturday night. Usually her two roommates were busy with work or hanging with their significant others, leaving little time for just the three of them to hang out together. Tessa dropped down onto the other side of the L-shaped couch, kicking off her shoes before tucking her feet under her. "Sure. Let me see what you have."

"Wait. Aren't you supposed to be on a date?" Anna asked, pulling the laptop back as she glanced over at Quinn, her gaze disapproving as she peered down at

Tessa through her tortoise-shell glasses. "What happened?"

"Nothing happened. I just didn't think it was going to work out between us is all, and I told him as much. Now don't give me that look. I'm not going to die alone." Although it sure had been feeling that way of late.

"You will if you don't put yourself out there," said Quinn.

"Lectured the pot to the kettle," Tessa said wryly. "You didn't find James because you were putting yourself out there. You were worse than me if I remember right. You just got lucky that your boss had the hots for you as much as you did for him."

"Well, we can't all be like Anna, fighting them off with a stick only to realize she'd hit the right one over the head back in high school."

"True," Anna, who had reconnected with her high school nemesis at her sister's wedding in June, said good-naturedly. They'd been going strong ever since. "In fact, for all you know, Tessa Montenegro, your Mr. Right isn't some complete stranger, but someone from your own past. Maybe some little boy whose butt you kicked on the playground."

Tessa laughed a little more nervously. There was no chance either of her friends could be referring to Dylan Jamison, because she had never shared with them the pain of what had happened between them, and the whole thing had happened well before she knew them. Tessa's friendship with the women had only begun after she met Quinn in their first year of law school and she moved in with them to escape from student housing. And even though they'd remained best friends and roommates ever since—something necessary with the skyrocketing costs of living in San Francisco and the abysmal income of two law school graduates and one wannabe reporter—she hadn't been able to bring herself to share this one personal thing with them.

"You know, you'd think with all that testosterone in your household growing up, they'd have one decent friend they could hook you up with," Quinn speculated.

"Are you kidding?" Tessa asked, hoping her voice sounded calmer than she felt. "The last thing my brothers would ever want is my hooking up with any of their friends. Which reminds me..." Tessa picked up her phone and scanned the incoming messages. "Finn texted me earlier asking that I call when I had a moment. Let me find out what's going on and then I'll read that story for you, Anna," she said and pressed his number on her phone as she headed to her room.

Finn answered immediately. "Hey. Thanks for calling back. We kind of have a situation. Dad fired the home nurse we had lined up for him. And the replacement who showed up today."

Her dad had only arrived home from the hospital two days ago. "You're kidding. Already? What happened?"

"Who knows. Well, actually, scratch that. It's Dad. You know how he can get. Not helped by the fact that his bedroom has been temporarily relocated to the sitting room."

"Yeah, I can imagine. How can I help?"

He sighed. "Okay, well, I wouldn't ask this of you unless I was out of ideas. And if it were any time of the year other than October, I'd be here, no problem. But the Cabernet grapes could be ready any moment, and you know how chaotic things get in the days leading up to that, and combined with the rest of the work on the farm, the apple harvesting, and my needing to get that first batch of cider ready for the Harvest Festival next weekend, I just can't do it all alone. Daphne's been doing what she can to help, but she's as tied up as I am. And with Declan at the fire station and Rowan's job and class schedule, there's no one here in the day to take care of him. Even Dylan has been trying to do what he can, but I hate to continue putting him out like that."

Finn was right. Her dad's care wasn't Dylan's responsibility. The guilt ripped through her. Yes, she had a job that was unforgiving of anyone taking any time off, let alone a full week without notice. But this was her dad. The guy who used to sit patiently for an hour's time while she drew his likeness for whatever new art project she was working on. Who'd made her a cup of tea the first time she came home heartbroken and in tears when Max Brody dumped her after the eighth-grade dance. Who had been right there to comfort her when a nightmare tore her awake in the middle of the night in those weeks after her mom died and Dylan left. He was always there for her when she needed him—even if she didn't think she did—and it was time for her to repay the favor.

"You're right," she told Finn, "Dylan shouldn't be dealing with this and you shouldn't have to bear the weight of this alone. I can be there tomorrow."

A few minutes later, plans in place, Tessa came out to the front room, where her roommates were watching television.

"Everything okay?" Quinn asked, pausing the stream.

"It will be." She relayed to them what was going on and how, at least for the next week, she needed to help her dad until he could do more things for himself, even if the prospect of talking to the senior partner about her unplanned absence made her stomach tie up in knots.

"You're making the right decision, Tessa," Anna said,

without hesitation. "Your dad needs you. Besides, you've been busting your butt at that firm for three years without taking one day of vacation. You're entitled to do so, especially for this."

"What do you think, Quinn?" Tessa asked, not that her friend's answer would change her mind, but it might help her feel better about the decision she was going to make, since Quinn, like Tessa, knew all too well the demands and expectations for new associates in large law firms, having been one herself once.

"I agree. You're doing the right thing for you. That's not to say that in the short term this might leave some people questioning your dedication, but once you're back at the office and kicking butt again, this will all be a distant memory."

Ted Larson, the senior partner on the project she was assigned, was not going to be happy, and she could imagine the judgment and contempt in his eyes at hearing her request to take time off. Heck, just last month, one of the second-year associates had to take time off for a burst appendix, and when he was ready to come back, Ted made him spend a full month with the first-years before reinstating him.

"Yeah. Let's hope so," she said not so confidently.

"In the meantime," Anna said, putting her hand over hers in a reassuring manner, "you're going to be where you need to be, taking care of your dad. Besides, I'd be curious if, after living with us for the past six years, you can survive being surrounded by all that male testosterone again."

They only knew the half of it. Sure, it had been easy for Tessa to pretend that having Dylan stay over at the house didn't bother her when she had no plans of staying in said house. But now that she was heading home, knowing she would run the risk of seeing him and his smug grin every time she stepped foot outside her door was another thing entirely.

"It's going to be worse than either of you could ever imagine."

THREE

It was late Sunday afternoon, and Dylan and Rowan were watching Finn as he opened the top of the tank that held one of the batches of cider. It had been a long process for Finn to even get to this stage, as he'd started out by selecting only certain varieties of apples from the early August harvest he thought would be optimal for taste. Then the apples had been pressed, the juice fermented with active yeast to turn the juice's natural sugars into alcohol. From that stage, he'd moved the cider into the current tanks to mature for anywhere from a few weeks to months, depending entirely on the flavor Finn was seeking.

Today's batch they were sampling had been maturing for six weeks already in preparation for their entry into next weekend's annual Blossom Falls Harvest Festival contest for Best Cider. The winner would be featured in several reputable magazines, including one of the West Coast's finest culinary magazines, something that could really help their company get off the ground.

Finn poured cider into three small tumblers and held one up to the early evening sun to analyze the color before bringing it back down. He inhaled the aroma as if savoring it before finally taking a drink. He sighed and looked expectantly at Dylan and his brother. "Well?"

Now, Dylan wasn't new to the tasting process. When he first arrived, Finn had wrangled him into trying several different varieties, and all of them at this stage had been dry and sour, the sugar from the apples all eaten by the yeast and turned into alcohol. So he wasn't that excited about trying this one. Rowan seemed to be of the same opinion as he stared at his glass. Not that that first sip had been terrible, but he'd been expecting it to be naturally sweet like the cider he drank as a kid, so the dry unsweetened flavor had been a shock.

But this was his business now, too. And this was part of the process. He tipped his glass to Finn. "Bottoms up," he said and took a drink, waiting for his mouth to pucker.

His eyes widened. No pucker, no dryness. Actually it was pretty good, a tiny bit sweet but also tangy.

"I thought this batch wasn't back sweetened," Dylan said, referring to the process Finn used in the other batches of adding a non-fermenting sugar to the dry brew to get the ultimate flavor he was seeking.

Finn's smile widened. "It wasn't."

Rowan, braver after Dylan's experience, threw his back, too. "Wow. That's a helluva lot better than I expected. What's different?"

Finn laughed. "I used some of the heirloom apples from the old orchard, the apples that aren't pretty enough for selling on the market. They're in their unaltered state verses a lot of the varieties available now that have been engineered for looks and high yield. Heirlooms have high natural non-fermentable sugars that aren't converted to alcohol, leaving a sweet flavor. Mix that with a selection of other varieties and you have this."

Dylan had known that Finn was a bit of a nerd when it came to farming and anything horticulturally related, but here it almost sounded like a mix of both science and art, which was impressive.

The familiar jingle from Dylan's pocket told him that his agent was calling. "I've got to grab this," he said to the brothers and ducked outside. "Hey, Larry."

"I wanted to check in with you, see how things are coming."

"You mean since I last saw you, what? Five days ago?"

"What can I say? I worry about you, kid." Larry paused and Dylan waited, knowing there was more. "Plus I was hoping that you might have changed your mind about performing with Roxie out in LA. We think it will do wonders in pushing your next album."

Dylan rubbed the back of his neck, trying for patience. No matter how many times he'd told his agent that he wasn't interested in pretending he and Roxie were still a thing, regardless of the frenzy it might send the tabloids into, the guy couldn't let it go. "I don't see it happening, Larry. Besides, if I don't keep my focus, there isn't going to be another album to sell."

"Well, keep it in mind. I know that Roxie would love to have you back in the night's lineup."

He'd just bet. At least for the promotion opportunity it would provide her. But seeing as how she'd already been seen out with the same bass player who he caught her with that night, he doubted she'd be heartbroken. "Sure, Larry. I'll talk to you later."

Dylan pocketed the phone, ready to return to the barn

when a plume of dust in the distance told him the Montenegros' next visitor's arrival was imminent.

Tessa was coming home.

He almost hadn't believed it when Finn told him about her decision. From what he'd heard, Tessa's visits home had been getting rarer and rarer, usually only saved for holidays and special events, what with her new life in the city and this job of hers. She had apparently become a city girl, which was the last thing he ever would have expected for her.

The blue Subaru came into view now, and he could make out Tessa's dark hair as she turned the car into a spot next to the house. He'd be lying to himself if he said the sight of her didn't bring an odd tightening feeling in his chest, an excitement that he repressed since he knew that those emotions were what got him into trouble ten years before. She was Finn's sister, an old family friend, and nothing more. There *couldn't* be anything more.

He made his way over to help her out. "So you made it," he said when she climbed out, taking a second to pop open the trunk.

"I made it. How couldn't I? Where is everyone?" she asked, looking up at the house and avoiding his gaze.

"Finn and Rowan are currently having a taste testing in the barn, Declan's running some errands before his next shift starts at the firehouse but he'll be here in time for dinner, and Daphne is inside getting dinner ready and watching out for your dad." He lifted her heaviest suitcase from the back of the car.

"You don't have to do that. I'm more than capable of getting it all in myself."

"I'm sure you are. But Daphne would have my hide if I left you doing all the heavy lifting."

"That's probably true," she said softly, as if conjuring a memory. "So. Has Dad really been as much a handful as Finn tells me?"

He paused. Joe Montenegro had been a father figure ever since Dylan first came to live with his aunt, never hesitating to include him in any of the family plans, welcoming him for dinner and any other events. Dylan owed him a lot. But...yeah. It hadn't been easy these past few days, with Joe more cantankerous than usual over the fact he couldn't do any of his usual chores and tasks by himself.

"I'll take it by your silence that it's affirmative," she said.

He shrugged, choosing to remain noncommittal. His gaze dropped to the smaller bag stuffed with files, legal pads, and the corner of a laptop peeking out, and he nodded toward it. "What's all that? I thought Finn said you were taking some vacation time."

"Let's just call it a working vacation."

He paused so she could get in front of him before following her up the walk, very aware of the way her denim cutoffs clung to the curves of her lower body. Instead of drawing his gaze away as he should if he wanted to retain any control over his sanity, however, he took the opportunity to appreciate the pint-sized woman's bold curves, the softness that was all too enticing.

Couldn't hurt to look, right?

He was in the middle of a slow smile when she whipped her head around to glance at him, almost as if she was sensing where his thoughts were, and he quickly dropped the grin and looked straight ahead.

Look but don't touch.

That was going to be a hell of a lot easier if he did a lot less looking—and a lot less getting caught.

Tessa was being ridiculous.

There was no way that heartthrob Dylan Jamison, a.k.a. Dylan Charles, had just been checking out her butt. She knew very well what her butt looked like, and rock star worthy it was not. At five foot two inches, she was half the height of all the willowy models he'd been photographed with over the years, making her legs stubs in comparison, and her butt cheeks undoubtedly doubly as soft. And yet... she'd gotten the distinct impression he'd been staring at more than just the back of her head.

Dylan's eyes crinkled up as if trying to figure out what was wrong, not a sign of guilt in their brown depths, confirming that Tessa's instinct had been wrong. It wouldn't be the first time her instincts had been wrong where Dylan Jamison was concerned.

"Sorry," she said, and grimaced, "I was trying to remember if I grabbed my cell phone, but"—she dug in her back pocket and pulled it out to keep up the pretense—"I've got it."

His annoying smile gave her the impression he didn't buy it. She turned back around and climbed the porch steps, anxious to get inside and away from his immediate line of vision. Opening the kitchen door, she was met with her dad and Daphne in the middle of an argument.

At seeing her, her dad smiled. Or attempted to smile. "Tessa, honey. I told those boys you didn't have to come."

"I know, but how could I resist the opportunity to spend some quality time with my dad? So, what are you two arguing about?"

Daphne rolled her eyes. "He wanted to carry the plates over to the table to set it and I refused to let him—"

"I'm more than capable—" he started saying from his seat at the kitchen table.

But Daphne continued speaking as if she didn't hear him, "—even though he knows perfectly well he's not supposed to lift or carry anything that weighs over ten pounds."

They glared at each other for another minute before her dad grunted and picked up the newspaper and shook it out, then buried his face into it.

Giving a sympathetic nod to Daphne, Tessa headed over to her dad and placed a kiss on his whiskered cheek. "Good to see you're still in good spirits," she teased him.

"I'm going to take your bags up," Dylan said, disappearing from the kitchen.

Tessa noted the crutches leaning against the wall next to her dad. "Are you feeling any better?"

"Considering I've been stuck in the house for the past three days with nothing to do, I've been better. The last thing I need is people mothering me—and that goes for you, too, honey. You know"—his tone softened—"I appreciate you coming out here, but like I told your brothers, there are more important things for you to be doing than nursing a grumpy old man. You'd be serving yourself better if you ate supper with us and then headed back home and to that job of yours. No sense putting it in jeopardy."

"I'm not putting it in jeopardy. I've got my laptop and an internet connection, so I can still keep up with what's going on at the office."

"Well, don't be getting it into that head of yours that I'm a complete invalid like that last daft nurse. I can pull my own shorts on and off without your help."

"Noted." Time to change the subject. "Something smells great. What are we having?"

Daphne smiled. "Salad with roasted garden veggies, garlic bread, and pasta carbonara."

"You're trying to fatten us all up, I see. Let me help set the table at least."

"It beats the takeout we've had for the past couple nights," Dylan said.

Tessa glanced up to see that in the space of time since he'd been upstairs, Dylan had changed into a clean, snug-fitting olive-green tee that enhanced the specks of gold in his brown eyes—not to mention the sinewy strength of his upper torso. She diverted her gaze and grabbed the salad, bringing it to the table.

The door opened and Finn and Rowan strode in, laughing at something as they stopped at the sink to wash up. "Hey, Tessa," they called in greeting when they spotted her.

"What were you guys doing out there?" Tessa asked, looking over her brothers, who were covered in dirt and sweat, their hair plastered to their heads. She fanned her hand in front of her nose as a whiff of eau de sweat and dirt reached her. "Did we take up pig farming and no one told me about it?"

Instead of looking insulted, Finn smiled widely at Rowan, both coming to an understanding as they drew closer. "Now is that the way to greet your two favorite brothers? Come on, give us a big old hug," Finn said, his arms outstretched.

She squealed and took a couple steps back only to be stopped by Rowan. "No. I was kidding. Don't even think—"

"Boys. Enough," her dad said just in time. "You are pretty ripe, so before you sit down to that table, you're going to need to do a little more than wash your hands."

Tess refrained from gloating as she watched her

brothers mosey out of the kitchen, smiling dangerously as they passed. She caught sight of Dylan, who shook his head at her, keeping his laughter in check if the shaking of his shoulders was any indication.

By the time Finn and Rowan returned, Declan had arrived and was already seated at the table alongside her dad and Daphne. He was dressed in his navy-blue firefighter uniform, clean-shaven and his hair trimmed and styled, and Tessa smiled as she thought about how far Declan had come from his days as the town troublemaker to become the town hero.

"You should have brought everyone a sampling of your latest creation, Finn," Rowan said, grabbing a beer from the fridge before sitting next to Dylan. "It's hands-down better than this."

"They'll get a chance soon enough," Finn said. "That is, if Tessa is still around for the Harvest Festival next weekend."

It had been years since she'd been in town for the annual festival. It had been one of her favorite events growing up, entering the pie-baking contest with her mom and the potato sack race with whichever brother she could guilt into teaming up with, and later munching on hot cider donuts and caramel apples until her stomach ached. Good times. "I'll try and fit it in my schedule. So what's the new recipe you've been working on? Dylan poured me a glass the other night and I have to admit, it was better than I remember."

"I've been working with some of the heirloom apples from the old orchard. I'm still perfecting things, but I think what I've got is pretty good," he said modestly.

"It's more than that. It's amazing," Rowan said. "You're sure to be the winner."

"Don't go jinxing us," Finn said, but she could see he was pleased. "It does have me wondering about expanding. The old Wallace place has been vacant for years, and their orchards date as far back as ours," he said, referencing the property that sat empty on the other side of the Montenegros' orchards. "It's a shame to see the apples just go to waste. Dylan and I were wondering if whoever owns the place now might be interested in selling."

Her dad considered it for a moment. "I think the place went to a sister who lives out in Pasadena. You might have luck checking with Jasper. He'll know for sure."

Dylan nodded. "I have an appointment with him tomorrow to talk about some other matters. I'll see what he says."

Other matters? She eyed him, trying to see if he was going to expand, but the talk was already moving on to something about meetings with suppliers. What kind of matters could Dylan have that needed the assistance of an attorney?

As if sensing she was observing him, he looked over and met her gaze. Immediately she felt that familiar flush of heat, and she ripped her gaze away, trying to pretend that nothing was out of the ordinary.

She wanted to kick herself. Why, after all this time, after everything she'd gone through when she lost him, was she still so susceptible to his charms?

She was going to need to toughen up if she had any hope of surviving the next week.

"So tomorrow," Daphne said later that night to Dylan as they walked the short distance to her place. "Big day."

"It should be."

"Have you given any thought as to what you'll do if you find out the little girl is Brick's daughter?"

His aunt was the only person he'd trusted with the information. It had seemed appropriate that she should know, considering if it was true, she would also gain a niece. Dylan had weighed the possibility of confiding in Finn, but he wanted to be sure of the relationship before he did so, feeling that if it was all a sham, it might be less painful to him the fewer people who knew.

"If it's true, I'll put together a support plan for her where she'll receive money every month to help her and her mom cover the bills." According to the private investigator he'd hired, Elle's mom was a single parent who worked double shifts at a diner in Santa Rosa just to support her daughter, while also squeezing in a couple courses at the community college. Even with the doubles, they were two months behind on the rent, and the only reason they hadn't been kicked out was because the old lady who owned the place had a soft spot for the duo. Dylan figured they deserved some good in their life and he could offer them that.

"That's not quite what I meant," his aunt said, keeping her attention on the road and the rocks and dips that could make the walk treacherous. "If she is your sister, have you thought about what that would mean to her? To you? You're going to need to decide how much you want to be in her life. If you decide you want to be a part of it, you can't just go and disappear, whether your accountant sends them that check or not."

"When I get to that bridge, I'll be ready to make that decision. And how about you?" he asked, glancing over.

She sighed and looked up at the stars. "I'll be there as

much as she'll want me to be. Just like I was for you." She was quiet for another moment. "I know you didn't know your dad and that's entirely his fault. He had big dreams, big ambitions, and sometimes he couldn't see beyond himself and his needs to those around him. He'd always been that way and I suppose being the apple of my mom's eye didn't help much in grounding him. But when all's said and done, he was my brother and I loved him, and I would want to make sure that his daughter was as well looked after as his son."

"She'd be lucky to get to know you," he said, pointedly refusing to discuss his old man. Brick Jamison had been selfish when he took off on Dylan and his mom, plain and simple. He didn't deserve any more space in Dylan's mind.

She wrapped an arm around his shoulder and pulled him in for a second before releasing him. "I was the lucky one when it came to you."

"That's not what you were saying back when I was collecting bullfrogs that summer."

"I don't know how you managed to keep it a secret for as long as you did. If I hadn't finally noticed my good China disappearing and gone looking for it in that room of yours, I can't imagine how much longer that stench might have stuck around."

"I think it was November before the swampy smell disappeared."

She chuckled. "Well, if your sister is anything like you, we're going to be in trouble. From the sound of it, traveling all that way to sneak backstage at a concert to see you, she might actually be *more* trouble."

They were silent for the next few minutes until they reached the cottage. "You'll let me know when you find out?"

"You'll be the first person I call."

She nodded, assured, and continued up the stairs to her small but tidy porch with a million-dollar view of the valley. He'd offered multiple times to do her place up right, give her at the very least an extra eight hundred square feet and a kitchen that didn't look like it hailed from circa 1965, but she'd refused him every time. This was her home, she'd said, and she didn't need any fancy doodads. Just more time with him.

"Now, go on. I can see myself inside. And try to stay out of trouble," she added.

"Trouble? You're talking like I'm some sixteen-year-old punk. What kind of trouble could I possibly get in?" he asked innocently.

"Don't make me spell it out for you. Just...be mindful of your actions, okay?"

She was clearly losing it, but he wasn't ready to push it and have her spell out whatever it was she thought she knew.

"Okay. I'll be mindful. Good night, crazy lady."

"G'night."

When Dylan reached the Montenegros' farmhouse a few minutes later, he stood outside looking up at Tessa's window, still alight from the lamp by her bedside.

He wouldn't feel guilt for what he did when he left all those years ago. He couldn't. Not when he knew that he'd done it for her own good. If he hadn't, what might have become of her waiting all those years for a guy who didn't deserve her? Would she be as successful as she was now? Or would she have become like that shell his mother had become after years of waiting for a man who never came back?

Tessa had been better off without him back then. He was sure of that.

Still...

He looked up at the stars, no doubt the same stars that had been above them that night. What would have happened had he kept that door open? Where would he be? Where would she be? Would they have made it?

Would she still think he was worth waiting for? He'd never know.

FOUR

Tessa woke up just after seven the next morning, a first for someone who was usually up and at work by that time. But after her first six hours on dad duty last night, she'd earned the extra time in bed.

She had been certain that her brothers were exaggerating about her dad's stubborn reticence to accept help, but after fighting him to do the stretching exercises his doctor prescribed, stopping him from doing his Sunday night tour of the farm on crutches that were bound to fumble over the gravely path that wound around the farm, and catching him —literally—as he tried to kick a basket of clothes down the hall in an attempt to do his own laundry, she'd been exhausted from her efforts.

She lingered in bed another moment, relishing the feeling of being home again. Enjoying the light that poured into her room through the light lavender gauzy drapes she'd chosen when she was fifteen, and the softness of the old quilt that had once been her mom's as she brought it up close to her face, almost imagining she could still smell her mom's scent.

The house was quiet, but from the sound of machinery outside the windows, the activity on the farm was going strong. She listened, trying to see if she could discern the whereabouts of the household, one inhabitant in particular who might be lingering about, but after a few minutes of complete quiet, she was certain the second floor was absent anyone but her.

Well, she wasn't going to hide in here all day. After throwing the covers off, she grabbed a few things and headed to the bathroom to shower.

"Morning, Dad," she said half an hour later as she slunk down the stairs and found him sitting in his easy chair reading the morning newspaper, something that was comforting in its tradition. She kissed him on his bristly and still unshaven cheek and headed to the kitchen to fix a quick cup of tea. "How long have you been up?" she called out.

"Usual time. Just after five."

"Everyone's already up and out of the house, I take it?" she asked, hoping she sounded only mildly interested in the answer.

"For a couple hours now."

That was something of a surprise to her since she would have thought rock stars like Dylan would be in bed until at least noon. She leaned against the doorway as she dipped the tea bag up and down in the hot water. "Are you hungry? Can I fix you anything?"

"Finn made breakfast first thing before heading out. Actually"—he paused and scratched his head as if it was only occurring to him—"I was thinking that maybe I could join him out in the fields for a little while. Make sure everything's on schedule for—"

"Not going to happen. You're only five days post-surgery and you need to be sure you don't do anything that would risk you falling and injuring yourself. Besides, you have your first visit from the physical therapist today, and we don't want you to be too tired to actually do the exercises you need to strengthen that hip."

"I have to have something to do with all this time on my hands. I'm not an invalid. A little sun on my face would be good for me."

She studied him, aware that, for a busy guy like her dad, staying anywhere stationary for any period of time had to be painful. "How about we see what your therapist says today? If she gives you the thumbs-up, then I won't stop you."

He grunted and turned his attention to the paper, his bifocals low on his nose as he peered down. For a man now in his early sixties, she had to hand it to him for still being something to look at, knowing that many of the women in this town had been hoping he might finally turn an eye in their direction in the years after her mom died.

His dark brown hair had wafts of gray strewn through especially around the brows, but it was still thick and wavy and something men half his age would envy. His face had always been handsome, and her brothers had been lucky on that end to have inherited his better traits, like his stubborn but strong jawline and well-formed facial structure, not to mention the strapping physique that came from growing up on a working farm and laboring under the warm California sun. It had also made her own childhood doubly challenging since she'd struggled to distinguish between the girls who were sincerely interested in being her friends and those who were more interested in dating one of her brothers.

Her dad shifted in his seat as if trying to get comfortable, flinching as he did.

"Have you had any pain meds today?"

He continued to read. "The pain is nothing I can't manage."

"At least let me get you a fresh ice pack. And maybe some Tylenol."

"If you insist."

She went back to the kitchen to retrieve ice and medicine, only to find when she returned that he'd nodded off in the chair. Quietly, she slipped back into the kitchen and put the ice back into the freezer. When he woke up, she could give him everything, but for now, he could probably stand the rest.

With some time on her hands, Tessa retrieved her work bag and laptop and took up a post at the kitchen table. It was insane the number of emails she accumulated when she wasn't obsessively checking and reading them as they came in, and it took her more than half an hour to sift through the ones she had in order of priority.

She was still working when the doorbell rang, announcing the arrival of her dad's physical therapist. After getting the two of them settled into a space in the living room that had been adapted to allow room for any exercises her dad needed, Tessa made a bid to get out of the house.

"If you're okay, I'm going to run out to refill your prescription and get a few things at the market," she said to her dad.

"I'll manage," he said irritably.

"We'll call you if we need anything," the physical therapist assured her, not seeming to be bothered by her patient's demeanor.

Tessa nodded and gave her dad a warning glance before returning to the kitchen to pack her work away. The back door opened just as she grabbed her phone, and Finn and Dylan walked in.

"Look who finally joined the living. You city girls sure like to spend your time in bed," Finn said, grabbing glasses for him and Dylan from the cupboard.

She ignored him. "I'm running into town if you could keep an ear out for Dad. He's with his therapist now."

"Sure," Finn said, chugging his water as Dylan leaned against the counter.

It was hard not to appreciate the sheen of sweat that glistened over Dylan's tanned forearms, the highlights that working out under the sun weaved into his dark blond hair that was all disheveled and messy.

"Actually, I was about to head to town myself," Dylan said with that smooth, drawling country-boy voice. "I have an appointment with your old employer. Why don't I give you a ride in? No sense in both of us driving separately."

Sit in a car alone with this guy? Not going to happen. "That's okay. Like I said, I have a few things to grab while I'm there and I don't want to keep you waiting. I'm sure you have a busy day scheduled."

"Nothing's on my schedule for the rest of the day. Besides, I could use the company."

Crap. She had no more excuses, and to continue to decline would only invite her brother's curiosity, who was already eyeing her as he finished his water. She nodded. "All right. But we probably should get going so I can be home by the time Dad's therapist leaves."

"I'm ready if you are. I'll drive."

"Fine." She led the way, stopping on the porch as she looked around, not sure what vehicle she was actually heading toward since the only ones there were her Subaru, Finn's Jeep, and the old Ford Truck at least ten years past needing a paint job. The same Ford where Dylan was opening the passenger-side door for her.

"You're kidding me," she said, her mouth hanging open. "This is what you're driving these days?"

He grinned. "I'm nothing if not humble."

Right. "So what kind of business do you have with Jasper anyhow?" she asked when they left the dirt road and turned out onto the highway, the radio softly playing a random country music station.

He didn't immediately respond, instead keeping his eyes on the road. "Just some personal stuff."

Helpful. It only served to increase her curiosity. But she knew that when he got that look on his face, he wasn't ready to open up. Not yet.

"Good old Jasper," she mused instead and stared outside at the hillside, a tapestry of rich colors as expected for October and the full swing of the harvest season. "Can't believe he's still in business after all these years."

When she was sixteen years old and needing a part-time job that didn't involve wading in six inches of manure-infused soils while plowing, planting, pruning, or ultimately helping in the harvest of the farm's various crops, Jasper's law office had been a great escape. She'd also found the work surprisingly fascinating. Being a small-town attorney, his practice ranged from handling the range of quiet to dish-shattering divorces of many of the town's inhabitants, writing up wills and real estate contracts, even defending the Fossie brothers when they were cited for lewd and inde-cent behavior after mooning the town's little league team after the playoffs. She never knew what would be his next case, and he was always willing to let Tessa learn and go as far as she could before taking over the reins.

It was that appreciation for the law that had given her some grounding, something new to aspire to that dark day when Dylan Jamison rejected everything she had to offer him and walked away. She'd left childhood dreams in the past and settled for reality. And she'd been perfectly happy with reality.

Until she found herself sitting next to the guy who still seemed to possess half of her damaged heart, who she hated with the fire of a million burning suns and yet couldn't stop staring at his fingers tapping gently against the steering wheel in tune to the song playing on the radio, and she was left remembering how it had felt for a blissful moment to have them touching her and holding her and making her feel...everything.

"Guess Jasper loves what he does. Makes it all the more rewarding," Dylan said, bringing her back to the conversation. "Don't you feel that way about what you're doing?"

Tessa thought about doing what she was doing for the rest of her life, and she couldn't strum up the same emotions. She always thought the work she was doing now was just temporary. Putting in the time and effort until she could move up to bigger and better things. "I will, eventually."

She sensed his gaze on her but she kept her attention outside the truck.

"I meant to ask you. What happened to your art? I remember a time when your art was everything to you. You could spend hours in front of a canvass, lost in the moment as you tried to capture a scene or a feeling. Hard not to notice that none of that seems to be part of your life anymore."

"There are a lot of things that aren't a part of my life anymore. That's what happens when you grow up. You leave those childhood dreams and foibles behind."

"Didn't think it was a foible, not for you."

"And how would you know?" she asked, her tone

sharper than she meant, but she couldn't seem to pull it back. "You don't know me. You don't know what I value in life, not anymore."

He nodded, appearing contrite. "Okay. Sorry, didn't mean to overstep."

She didn't want to talk about that part of her life. Sure, there were times when she caught the sun hitting the bay in the early evening and she wondered how she would capture the colors, what shades she'd blend to get the light just right. Or she'd be sitting on the couch, chatting with her roommates, a pencil in her hand, halfway through a sketch capturing the expression on Quinn's face as she prepared for her next trial, or Anna as she tried to get a sentence just right on a story, before she knew what she was doing. But she never got carried away enough to pull the brushes and oils out again. "I'm sorry, I didn't mean to bite your head off."

He touched his head. "Still intact. I'm not as sensitive as I might seem."

"Seems so," she said, her eyes drawn to that darn bicep again. Biceps that, now that she thought about it, seemed oddly unadorned. "How come you don't have a myriad of tattoos all over you? Isn't that par for the course for rock stars?"

He shrugged. "Haven't found anything worth inscribing permanently on my body."

She studied him, a memory coming back of Dylan hiding for more than two hours from his aunt because he refused to get his vaccinations, necessary for his first day of junior high. It took signing him up for guitar lessons to get him to finally relent. "You sure it doesn't have anything to do with your fear of needles?"

He smiled over at her, his brown eyes warm. "Forgot

how much you could remember. But like I said, if I found something worth inscribing, I'm sure I would be able to handle it."

She smiled. "Oh, of course."

On the radio, a familiar tune started playing, and a strong female voice that they both had to recognize started to play. She glanced over to Dylan, curious to see his reaction to the sound of his ex-girlfriend's voice. But his face didn't give anything away as he continued to drive.

"We can change the station if you want," she volunteered.

"Doesn't bother me."

Tessa thought about their conversation the other night when she'd pretended she didn't follow his personal business, using her friend's fandom as her excuse for knowing about his breakup, but she knew very well that wasn't the case. She had needed to know what happened between them, especially after months of seeing their happy faces smiling at her from the pages of *People* and all the other celebrity magazines, with the conjecture that the two were soon fated to be heading down the aisle.

And now, she could find out. Even if just to appease her roommates' curiosity. "Roxie seems pretty nice. A tad high maintenance, but nice."

He laughed. "Yeah. You could definitely call Roxie high maintenance." He glanced over at her. "So what do you want to know?"

"Is it true you two were practically engaged?"

"That's what my agent and everyone else would have liked you all to believe, but no. We weren't that kind of a relationship."

That was an odd thing to say. "That kind of relationship?" she repeated. "What kind were you? Because from the photos I saw, you two seemed to be pretty close." Oops. She'd revealed too much, but fortunately he didn't seem to notice.

"Sure, we dated. It was a good fit at the time. We both wanted the same thing, both were focused on our careers, and we didn't take anything too seriously. Until suddenly she did, and when I didn't give her the response she liked, she decided to punish me for it."

"It's true then?" she asked, her eyes bugging out of her head. "She and that guy hooked up?"

He gave her a side-eyed glance. "If the scene I walked in on was any indication, then yes."

"Oh. I'm sorry. That must have been awful for you."

"It definitely didn't do my ego any good. But I think my agent had the hardest time with it. Roxie Mann definitely brings with her drama and attention, thanks in no small part to her massive social media following. Can't say I miss the limelight that followed our every move when we were together. It's kind of peaceful once you're out of that world. Being here in Blossom Falls these past couple of weeks has helped me maintain a low profile, much to my agent's chagrin. He's on my case to show up at her final show in LA in a couple weeks, as we'd planned before the breakup."

"He wants you back together, despite what she did?"

"I don't think he cares if we reconcile or not. He wants the feeding frenzy that will descend on us as people wonder if we have. It's all about selling me and that next album. But I can't fault him for that. It is what I pay him for, keeping his eye on the crap I don't have the stomach for. And how about you?"

"What about me?" she asked, playing dumb, since she had some suspicions what he meant.

He gave her a look that told her he didn't buy it. "No boyfriend waiting for you back in San Francisco?"

She gazed out the window, remembering her conversation with Eric from the other night. "No boyfriend."

There was a pause and she sensed him studying her. "Any strong contenders over the past ten years?"

Strong contenders? She thought about Eric, and Josh and Rick before him. All nice guys, but there just didn't seem any point in pursuing anything, not with her busy schedule. She shrugged. "My schedule doesn't really provide a lot of time for dating. Maybe in a couple of years, once I'm more established, I'll have the luxury of long, leisurely weekends with someone."

"You sound about as bad as me," he said.

"Oh, no. You date, all right. I've seen the photos to prove it. You just can't bring yourself to commit."

"Is that right? I didn't think you followed that kind of stuff."

Busted. "It's hard to miss when it's staring at you in the checkout at the grocery store."

"Sure," he said, slowing the truck as they neared an open parking spot in front of Cooper's Market and pulled in.

After unbuckling, she climbed out, meeting him on the sidewalk. "I don't think I should be too long," she said. "I just have to run to the pharmacy first and then pick up a few things at the market."

"No worries. I don't know how long I'll be at Jasper's, but if you finish before me, you should come by. I bet Jasper would love to see you."

"I'll keep that in mind." With a wave, she turned to go, pausing for a moment to watch as he headed down the sidewalk, following his progress longer than she should have.

Ten years ago, he was still growing into the man he would become, his slim build sinewy but strong. And now... He was definitely doing something right.

She remembered the straggly, stubbly growth that he'd proudly let grow out on his chin when the first rush of testosterone hit around sixteen that today was full and thick and glorious and made her wonder if it was as soft as it looked. Not a full beard yet, but the growth of someone who was taking a break from the world.

A group of young teenaged girls stopped in their tracks as they saw Dylan before racing forward with their phones. He stopped to greet them and leaned in as they appeared to take a selfie then continued on his way.

She shook her head. If that was his idea of low profile, then she could only imagine what it would be like to be high profile.

A minute later, she walked into Harry's Pharmacy. It had been in Blossom Falls since before Tessa was born, having become an institution to the town for decades. She remembered coming here with her mom and being offered a lollipop after waiting patiently for whatever prescriptions were being filled.

Virginia Henley was at the counter today, finishing up a sale when she saw Tessa. Her face brightened into a smile as she greeted her. "Why, Tessa Montenegro! You're looking so darling these days. I love your haircut. How are you?"

"I'm doing fine, Virginia. How are you?"

"As well as you could expect. You did hear that Curtis and I divorced last year? Leaving me a free agent again. How is your dad doing? That was a nasty accident, and I've missed seeing that handsome face of his around here. Not that I don't appreciate seeing those fine brothers of yours coming in here, but your dad always had his charming ways."

He had? Her dad was more a curmudgeon than a charmer, but she nodded as if she agreed. Virginia Henley was somewhere in her late fifties and, even before she and Curtis split up, had always had a thing for her dad. "Speaking of whom, I understand you have a couple of his prescriptions ready to pick up?"

"We sure do. Hold on a second," she said and walked over to the shelves and started scanning items. "Did you hear about Claudia Nunn?"

Claudia? That was a name from the past. "No. What about Claudia?" Tessa asked.

"It looks like, after all these years, she's going to be forced to close up that art studio of hers. The gas company has been wanting to update some of its pipelines and has decided the path of the new pipes needs to go right where the studio is located on the back corner of her property. Something domain is what they call it."

"Eminent domain," Tessa corrected. Something a government entity could legally do if they deemed the taking of the land served a public interest.

Probably somewhere in her sixties by now, Claudia had always been one of the town's artsy hippies who made the place more unique, friendly, and eccentric. She'd offered community art classes for decades in a large shed in her backyard that she'd restored into something of an art studio. It was where Tessa had first held a paint brush, first heard the encouragement and nurturing she needed from an impartial observer that led her to believe maybe she had some talent. She owed Claudia a great deal in offering the one medium that had helped Tessa express her angsty teenage emotions as she grew up.

"That's terrible. Do you know if she's fighting it or if she has an attorney at least?"

Virginia brought the two bottles forward and started ringing them up. "I expect she's probably been in touch with Jasper. He handles most things like that around here, as you probably remember."

She did, of course, which was why working for the man had always been so interesting. Unlike now, when she could pretty much run rote on the steps each project was going to take, with few variances.

The door opened and Tessa glanced over to see the gaggle of girls who'd nearly mobbed Dylan earlier. They stopped at the front counter, where Harry's Pharmacy always stocked a wide array of candy and locally made treats, their excited voices impossible not to hear.

"Can you believe that he's still here?"

"And smoking hot. I wonder if he has a girlfriend, like one of those supermodels he's always photographed with. Do you think he and Roxie will get back together?"

"That's what I read. Maybe she'll come and visit him here!"

That was Tessa's cue to exit. "Thanks, Virginia."

"No problem, sweetie. And you be sure to tell your Dad hello for me."

"Sure will."

DYLAN STARED at the paper in front of him, not sure he was reading the results correctly. He glanced up at Jasper, who was sitting across from him. "And how accurate do you think this is?"

"Well, it's not as accurate as, say, a paternity test. But

there are shared markers that indicate a strong likelihood that you and this little gal are related. It's up to you to decide if that's enough."

"Did they get a copy of this report?"

"Delivered this afternoon," Jasper said.

A little sister. He still couldn't wrap his head around it. His entire life, he'd always felt a little lost, a little lonely, even after his aunt took him in and he became close to the entire Montenegro brood. He knew he would never have the same shared life experiences that, say, Tessa and Finn had, something he was always envious of. With a dad who'd taken off on him well before he'd ever formed a memory of him and a mom who was only devoted to her next hit until she overdosed, leaving him an orphan at twelve, he'd figured he was and always would be alone.

At least until that August night when a spunky red-haired girl with more determination than smarts had tracked him down. He hadn't quite believed her. Not until she showed him the picture.

The bell at the front door of Jasper's office jingled, bringing him from his thoughts, and he heard the receptionist greet the newcomer. Tessa was here already? How had time gotten away from him so quickly?

"Can we keep this between us?" he asked the attorney, even though he knew that, attorney-client privilege or not, Jasper would never betray his trust.

"I'm not telling a soul."

"You'll work up that contract for me? I want to make sure they're provided for."

"Of course, Dylan. As to the other matter, I'll start digging to see who holds the current title to the Wallace place."

"Thanks," Dylan said, coming to his feet and following

the older man out of the office and into the reception area, copies of the DNA test clamped in a folder in his hands.

"Tessa Montenegro," Jasper said in obvious delight as he greeted his past ingénue, who was seated at a chair near the entrance. "What an unexpected surprise. What brings you to my office today? Did you finally decide to accept my open invitation to turn your back on the big city and come home to our little piece of heaven to work?"

"You'd be the first person I'd come to, Jasper," Tessa said and smiled broadly before getting up to give the old man a hug, standing on tiptoe as she did so.

Hmph. Not quite the homecoming he'd received. Not that he could blame her, he supposed, since she'd been nearly naked at the time. A thought that brought an immediate smile to his lips despite his somber mood.

With her attention on Jasper, Dylan had an opportunity to study her unobserved. Her dark chin-length hair waved around her head, more tamed now than after her long car ride yesterday, giving her the appearance of sweetness with undercurrents of sexy. Full lips that he remembered feeling so soft and enticing under his even to this day swept wide into a smile that brought out the warmth in those green eyes.

"That's right. I heard about your dad's accident. How's he doing?" Jasper asked.

"He's on the mend but still as stubborn as ever. Which is why I guess they called me. They were all kind of hoping I could sweet-talk him into being a more...flexible patient."

Jasper chuckled. "Well, you do have your ways. I'm sure that your dad is happy to have you back, regardless of the reason. Will you be here long?"

Her eyes jumped over to Dylan for a moment and quickly back to Jasper. "A week if I'm lucky. Just enough time to allow Dad to get a little firmer on his feet and get his doctor's clearance at his visit next Monday. Actually, there was something I wanted to ask you about. I was over at the pharmacy earlier and Virginia mentioned that Claudia Nunn was losing the art studio. Something about the gas company needing the land for some new pipelines."

Jasper's face grew serious. "Afraid so. It will be a shame to lose that space after all these years."

This was news to Dylan. "Doesn't seem really fair," he said. "They can do that? Just come in and take her land without her having any say?"

"If it's for a necessary public purpose, they can," Jasper said. "But don't worry yourself about it. Claudia has since made peace with it. In fact, she'll end up with a tidy sum based on the recent appraisal we commissioned. Just have to come to an agreement on the final numbers with the gas company."

"You know," Tessa said, "I'm not an expert, but my practice does focus on real estate transactions. If you feel like running any legal arguments past me, maybe I can help."

"I think we're past that. But I can pass on your offer to Claudia next time I see her if you like."

Tessa nodded, not looking any more satisfied with Jasper's answer than before, even as she pinned a smile on and waved good-bye, promising to come see Jasper before she left town.

They were quiet as they reached the sidewalk again. "It really bothers you about Claudia, doesn't it?" he asked.

"It's just that the studio gave me and so many other kids so much over the years. It's a shame that the town is going to lose such a treasure."

"I wasn't very good at the art stuff when Aunt Daphne signed me up, but it was the first place I ever heard classical music like Debussy and Mozart, Beethoven and Tchaikovsky. Not to mention Dylan, the Beatles, and Simon and Garfunkel."

"I remember," she said softly, the warmth in her eyes as she studied him making his breath catch before she turned away.

"Who knows," he said, wanting to cheer her up. "Maybe something will pop up in the community that will offer the same opportunity. I mean, if Blossom Falls can host a yoga studio and an artisan cheese shop, then there's hope for a musical art studio."

She smiled. "It's crazy how things can change and yet somehow stay the same, isn't it?"

Her smile was infectious, and he wanted nothing more than to steal a little more of her company, even for just a few minutes. "Why don't we stop at the cheese shop, maybe sample a few flavors? I hear they have a frozen custard counter."

Tessa paused, looking ahead to the aforementioned store. The smile on her face slipped away, and something changed in her mood. A coolness that seemed to over-shadow the moment as she shook her head. "Sorry. I should get back to my dad. Not to mention I have a couple of bags of frozen items melting inside the truck."

"Some other time then."

"Sure. Some other time," she said in a manner that told him not a chance in hell.

Probably for the best. As she said, she'd be gone in another week, and they'd both get back to the normalcy of their separate lives.

FIVE

Tessa couldn't sleep. Whereas any other night the chorus of crickets outside her window would be a soothing and comforting refrain, tonight it was one more thing she couldn't shut out. Like the memory of Dylan's smile when she was trying to talk to Jasper, his brown, almost tawny eyes shining with a hint of curiosity and joy that had made her stomach twist and dance just like it did when she was a kid and had his attention, even if only momentarily.

Why was it that just standing one minute in his presence could so easily erase the past ten years of bitterness and pain? Her heart obviously hadn't learned its lesson, but her head had and she wouldn't let anything else below her neck sway her again. Not her heart. Not her stomach, and certainly not any parts farther south.

Gah! This is insanity.

She threw her covers off and squinted around the moonlit room for her slippers. A glass of milk and maybe a tiny slice of the apple cobbler she'd made for dessert were what she needed.

At the top of the stairs, she paused as she heard the murmur of male voices coming from the kitchen. Was that Dad and...Dylan?

She should just go right to bed. No sense inviting more of those lazy, crooked grins that would only make sleep harder to find. But curiosity kept her feet moving until she was standing in the kitchen doorway trying to figure what the two men could possibly be discussing in the middle of the night.

She spotted the checkered board laid out in front of them. "I should have known," she said, and stepped toward the table, confirming her suspicions. "Chess. You do know what time it is, right?"

They looked up guiltily. Her dad spoke first. "Dylan's been kind enough to keep me company these past few nights. Seeing as how sometimes I get restless with the pain and can't sleep."

"Why didn't you wake me?" she asked, concern for his health making her forget about the bulk of the other man watching her carefully. "Do you need one of the pain pills? The doctor said you can take it as needed."

He waved his hand. "Nah. I hate how that stuff makes me feel. I had some Tylenol, so that's as good as anything.

She came over and studied the board. "Who's winning?"

"Me. But only because I think your dad is setting me up for something I can't see," Dylan said.

Tess smiled and headed to the fridge. Good to hear she wasn't the only one who her dad always seemed to stay ahead of in the game. "Anyone want me to dish them up some cobbler?" she asked, spooning a healthy serving onto a plate.

"Sure, since you're offering," Dylan said.

"None for me, hon. That physical therapy session took more out of me than I thought. Do you mind if I turn in early tonight, Dylan?"

"No complaints here. I prefer the game ending when I'm still ahead."

"You're getting the hang of it, don't you worry," her dad said and started to pick up the board.

Dylan put his hand out to stop him. "I got this. You get your rest."

Tessa set a piece of the cobbler in front of Dylan just as her dad grabbed his crutches and started to stand. She rushed over to help him but he waved her away. "No, I've got it. I'll see you two tomorrow."

Tessa waited until his crutches were firmly gripped in his hands before leaning in to hug him. "Night, Dad," she said, trying not to help him to bed since, as he'd firmly made clear last night, he wasn't an invalid and he sure as hell could pull his own pants on and off without his daughter's help.

Returning to the counter, she covered the cobbler and put it in the fridge. She hesitated as she reached for the milk. Come to think of it, tea sounded better. Shutting the door, she grabbed the kettle from its place on the stove and filled it up, ever mindful of the man sitting behind her.

"Care for a game?"

A game of chess with Dylan? No way. That would involve too much time in between moves, time that would leave her studying the most inane things about him, like the cadence of his breath or the way he might lick his lips as he considered his move. All of which would undoubtedly leave her heart thrumming in her chest. No chance. "Probably not if I want to be asleep before one in the morning."

"Fair enough. But I'm guessing you're down here

because you weren't able to sleep. Maybe needed a distraction?"

She looked sharply at him. He couldn't possibly know what she'd been thinking about upstairs, the moments she'd been reliving. Keeping her voice even, she replied, "Just a lot on my mind. Nothing that a cup of tea won't help."

Dylan placed the cover over the game and moved it to the sideboard before grabbing the deck of cards. He started to shuffle. "Once upon a time, I remember you used to play a mean game of Speed. Even declared yourself the champion."

Instead of joining him at the table, she dug into her cobbler standing at the counter, trying to tamp down the competitive spirit that had her biting at the bit to prove her worth. In law school, she'd managed to hold her own against her roommates, even when they were deep into a second bottle of wine.

"Not scared of a little competition, are you?" he taunted.

Her gaze was drawn to the deft way his fingers shuffled and maneuvered the cards as he talked, quick and sure. Another reminder of how, despite her best efforts, being around Dylan was like an aphrodisiac that she couldn't resist.

And yet...she really did love that rush of adrenaline at whipping the cards down at lightning speed and leaving her competition in the dust, their frustration at being bested making her victory only sweeter. And it would be particularly satisfying if the person left in the dust were Dylan.

"All right. I guess a game or two won't hurt."

Grabbing her plate, she came to the table to join him as he dealt the cards. She took another bite, enjoying the sweet and fragrant taste of the fresh apples and cinnamon.

"You ready?" he asked, his first five cards drawn and ready to be played, his other hand, like hers, on the play cards waiting to be flipped over.

"Go," she said, flicking her wrist at the same time.

Queen. Grabbing the jack in her hand, she played her card and the next one, pulling new ones from her pile as quickly as she could, aware of Dylan doing the same. When they couldn't play more on the last displayed cards, they repeated it all, her blood racing as she did. His hand grazed hers more times than she could count, each touch making the action even headier.

She was down to just a handful of cards, and a glance at his hand showed the same, and the high stakes of winning this one had her ready to jump from her seat. The teakettle started to hiss, gradually increasing to a whistle, but there was no way she was stopping now. She met his gaze as they each placed their hand on the next card, ready to flip it.

An ace. Just what she needed, but she saw him move toward the same card, and she moved quickly, sliding hers under his, a moment she took to savor as she glanced up at him. Two seconds later, the piercing whistle from the kettle too loud to ignore, she'd won.

She threw her hands up in the air. "And that's how it's done."

He laughed, shaking his head. "Only because you shoved my hand out of the way at least three different times, you big cheater."

She ran to the stove to take the kettle off. "Please. Your big man-paws were blocking me almost the entire game. But if you need another round to help you realize that I'm the master, then go ahead and deal again," she said, dropping the tea bag into the cup and bringing it to the table.

Three rounds later, they were tied. This time she was

shuffling the cards. Her high from before was still soaring as was her anxiety level.

"You sure you want to go down in flames like this, Tessa? We could call it a wash and you could return to your bed still under the delusion you're the queen of the game."

"Please. If you would stop hovering over the cards, I might be able to actually see them as they're played." She dealt the cards slowly this time, saving her energy for the final found. Taking the top five of her cards, she arranged them in her hand before glancing up at Dylan. He was watching her with that warm glint in his eyes that caused her breath to catch in her throat.

"You really are beautiful, you know."

She nearly dropped her hand. No. This was what he wanted, to distract her. "Nice try, buddy. You're not throwing me off my game at this point."

He smiled, shaking his head. "I wouldn't dream of it."

But he still hadn't stopped staring at her, and she could feel her face growing warm. Dang it. She wouldn't let him get to her. She breathed in and exhaled slowly. Focus.

She nodded slightly as they flipped the top cards over and the game was in motion. Meaty paws again kept her from getting her cards down first.

"Stop it," she said, half-frustrated and half laughing as he seemed to know what he was doing. His hands were warm and slightly rough against her own skin, but she pushed back, not willing to let him take up all the space.

She leaned forward with two cards left in her hand as Dylan played down his last few cards. For a moment, he looked up and hesitated, giving her the opening she needed to push her cards down, playing off the run he'd started.

Victory.

Only, the look in his eyes was anything but defeated.

No, they were bright and heated as he met her gaze after a long moment. She glanced down, horrified when she saw that her shirt had slipped down to reveal more skin than she'd intended. Hastily she yanked it up, even as another kind of fire altogether took hold of her, making her skin feel sensitive and heated.

His eyes held hers, and the very air seemed to crackle with an intensity that had her heart about to beat from her chest.

The slamming of the kitchen door sent her leaping nearly a foot in the air.

"You two are still up?" It was Rowan.

Heck. What time was it? He was usually off from his shift at the restaurant at two.

Sure enough, the clock on the microwave told her it was well past that hour. She scurried to her feet. "Not for long. I just had to beat Dylan in a few hands of Speed. And with my title still secure, I think I'll retire for the night."

"Yeah, I could have told you that would happen, bro. Tessa can be a tad over-competitive when it comes to cards."

"You're one to talk," she scoffed, since, being the youngest brother of five, Rowan seemed to feel he had something to prove, much like her.

"It will certainly be my pleasure to topple her reign one of these times," Dylan drawled. "She can't stay on top forever."

Her stomach seemed to be melting at the implication, even though she was almost certain she was imagining it. Just in case, she refused to look at him again, refused to see that boyish grin spread across his face at her expense. "There's cobbler in the fridge if you want any," she said to Rowan and raced out of the kitchen, calling over her shoulder, "See you guys in the morning."

A few minutes later, she was back in her own bed, no closer to sleep than she had been when she left two hours before for a nightcap. If anything, sleep felt impossible, her treacherous body still warm and tingling as she relived the moments in the kitchen.

So much for mind over matter.

Her mind was definitely lost.

"CARE FOR A TOPPER?" the waitress asked Dylan, the pot of coffee already hovering midair.

He nodded, careful to push his cap farther down on his head, etiquette be damned. The last thing he wanted right now was to be identified, thus ending his covert operation here. "Thanks."

The waitress left without any indication she knew who he was, leaving him to his surveillance. According to Jasper, Lana Buchnell, mom to the irrepressible Elle Jamison, had accepted the courier's delivery with the test results the day before. So his arrival here shouldn't be too much of a shock to her.

All the same, he'd wanted to observe her first. He tried to tell himself it was because he wanted to see what kind of a woman was raising his sister, but the fact was that he wanted to know what kind of woman it took to capture the heart of his old man.

Would she be a shadow of a woman, broken and dejected, like his own mom? Would she have the same slight build and soft blue eyes? Or would she be of sterner stock, not one to fall apart at his abandonment, staying strong if only to raise her young daughter?

He'd only been here twenty minutes, but in that space

of time, he could see that Lana Buchnell wasn't anything like his mom. From all appearances, Lana hadn't let Brick Jamison's abandonment break her. Of average height and weight, she bore no markers that made her stand out from everyone else save for the bright red of her hair. Her smile was as warm as one could expect from a woman who spent easily ten hours a day on her feet carrying heavy trays and filling endless cups of coffee. He had to give it to her, though. Beneath the fatigue and sadness that seemed to linger around her eyes, he sensed a woman who was stronger and more capable than people gave her credit for.

For the moment, Lana was in the kitchen and out of sight. Stifling a yawn, Dylan grabbed his coffee cup, needing the fortification. Usually he and Joe Montenegro would play chess until around midnight, when his mind would finally be too tired and spent to think about his problems. But last night, playing cards with Tessa had been anything but cathartic or relaxing.

It had been exhilarating.

Watching her face flush with either victory or frustration, her green eyes sparkling with excitement as she plowed through her hand, had been a joy. But it also had left him with a million thoughts—half of them which would leave his body bruised and pummeled if her brothers got any inkling of those thoughts—running through his head until the sound of the rooster outside his window told him he might as well just embrace the new day.

So after having an early breakfast with Finn and some of the crew and then lending a hand with the morning chores, he'd called Jasper to see if he'd heard anything from Lana and Elle, only to be told Lana had returned the check Dylan sent via the same courier. Dylan had headed directly here.

The table Lana had been covering finally left, and as if sensing the vacancy, she came out of the kitchen and busied herself cleaning it off, pocketing what looked like a lousy five bucks even though the bill had to be well over fifty dollars. It was only when she finished and stood upright that he was able to catch her gaze. He saw immediately the moment of recognition as the faint smile she'd worn slipped away and her eyes narrowed.

She headed over. "What are you doing here?" she hissed.

Dylan made his pitch as quickly and efficiently as he could. That he wanted to make sure that his sister had the things she needed since it wasn't her fault she'd been stuck with such a loser of a father who'd bailed on her and his responsibilities.

If he'd hoped that lambasting his old man might glean her trust or at least a shared interest as it used to with his mom, he was mistaken, as her back stiffened and the woman, if anything, seemed more affronted than before.

"I know you think you mean well, but let me disavow you of any impression you might have of me or my daughter. I'm not looking for any handouts, never was and never will. Elle took it upon herself to go out to LA to see you, and I grounded her soundly for a month afterward. She's not looking for a handout, either. She only wanted to know you, to feel a connection to you since, with Brick gone, you're all she has left of her father. Something that you made clear to her you weren't interested in. As to your father, well, that's a story for another day, but you should know he did the best he could. We might not have been right together, but his leaving was as much my fault as it was his. And with his passing, I would hope you would find it in your heart to forgive him."

"Lana? Order four is ready and table three needs to order still," the heavyset guy called from behind the grill.

"Be right there," she said and scurried over to take care of her customers.

When she approached him again, she seemed wary but resigned to finishing the meeting.

He tried again. "I'm only here because I care about Elle and want to help. I know you work fifty plus hours a week at this diner and you're trying to raise a daughter and take night courses at the community college. I know that you're barely making ends meet and that you're two months behind in your rent and the old lady next door who you pay to watch Elle is almost eighty and nearly too old to take care of herself, let alone a twelve-year-old girl. I just want to help out because, well, she's my blood. And if I can help her life be a little easier, I'd like to."

"Well, I thank you for the offer, but I'm afraid I'm not interested. Elle and I have gotten along just fine over the years, and we'll continue to without your help. Can I get your check for you?" she asked with a little more force.

"Sure." He knew that he'd said about all he could today. Not that he was going to give up just yet. He pulled a twenty for his meal along with an envelope from his pocket that he left on the table. "It's just a contract and outline of what I want to do," he said when she eyed the envelope like it was a poisonous snake. "You don't have to accept it, but could you at least look it over for me? Please?"

She nodded stiffly, not making a move to take the envelope that he left on the table. But at the door, he glanced back and saw with relief that she'd picked up the envelope and folded it before placing it in her pocket.

That would do. For now.

SIX

Tessa was back at the kitchen table by ten the next morning, her laptop on the table in front of her. Her dad was out in the barn keeping Finn company as he worked on the cider, leaving the house to her for a little while. She'd slept in again this morning, something that she was starting to enjoy, just like the relaxing cup of tea she'd had with her toast as she read the news from her phone instead of racing into work.

Dylan was already gone, off doing who knew what. Not that she cared. He was free to do whatever he wanted. Preferably far away from her.

She opened her email and got to work on the avalanche of emails she expected to have arrived since yesterday.

Hmm. Not nearly as many as she feared. Most of the messages she could easily respond to, but there were a few that she kept so she could respond more in depth. Busy work. That's what it was, nothing inspiring or exciting, just stuff that had to get done. Vacation or no.

She started to notice a trend in the emails as she got further in. Some of the earlier ones that she'd typed a quick reply to had already been answered by other associates at the firm. Questions sent to her began to be answered by others. It was a pointed reminder that she was but one cog in the wheel of the big machinery of a large law firm.

Nothing she did was particularly unique, and if she didn't get to it in the quick, timely fashion the firm expected, the request went to someone else with the same knowledge, same skill, same pay grade. Ultimately, she and her work were replaceable.

It was kind of...depressing.

Without guilt, she closed her email and opened up a fresh search page. She might as well make use of her time and see what she could do to help Claudia with her situation. It also helped to serve as a distraction from certain memories involving one Dylan Jamison and the fire in his eyes as he'd stared at her last night. She wasn't very successful on either score, unfortunately.

Don't be stupid, Tessa. How many other mornings had she spent growing up at this very table all moony-eyed and hopelessly lost in thoughts about Dylan Jamison? It hadn't done her any good then, and it certainly wouldn't do her any good now. It was wasted energy.

And yet, there was no denying that, whenever she got around the guy, she forgot the years of hurt and disappointment her infatuation had cost her, and she was living in the moment, awash with a stupid glow of contentment at having his attention, no matter how short.

There was a creaking outside the kitchen door, and Tessa sat up higher to peer out the window. But she didn't see anything.

Probably a rabbit or gopher or something.

A second later, the creaking returned, only this time there was a hesitant knock on the back door.

Getting up from her seat, Tessa headed to the door, curious who would be coming out here for a visit before noon as she opened it.

A young girl with red hair pulled into a straggly pony-tail stood before her. It seemed late in the season for Girl Scout cookies. "Hi. Can I help you?"

The girl kicked her shoe at the ground and peered up. "Um. Yeah. I was trying to see if Dylan was here."

Tessa studied the girl, who couldn't be older than thir-teen, trying to see if she recognized her or who she belonged to. But she'd spent far too many years away from the town to accurately predict her familial roots, even with the bright red of the girl's hair and the freckles sprinkled across her cherubic face.

Tess would venture a guess that she was a diehard fan of Dylan Charles trying to get a moment with the rock star. "Dylan isn't here right now, but..." Tessa paused when she heard a car engine and looked up to see a small sedan turning around and heading back down the road to the high-way, leaving the girl behind. "Wait. Is that your ride? Because I'm not sure how long it will be until he's back, so you might want to call them back."

"No. It's okay. It's just an Uber. Can I wait for him here?"

Wait for Dylan here? The last thing Tessa wanted to do was babysit a young fan who was waiting for Dylan. "Um, the thing is, I don't know how long he'll be. For all I know, he won't be back until tonight. Is there someone you can call to pick you up?"

The girl looked guilty as she glanced side to side. "No."

"What's your name, sweetie?" Tessa asked, a low level of panic beginning to fester as she tried to figure out what she was going to do with the girl. It had been some time since she'd been around an adolescent girl, probably since she'd been one.

"Elle."

"Okay, Elle. Maybe I can call your mom or dad and have them come get you. Do they live in town?" Another headshake. "Where are you from?"

"Santa Rosa."

Santa Rosa? "That's quite a trip for a young girl all by herself."

"I'll be thirteen in two months," she said, sounding offended at the accusation of being young.

Right. First thing to remember was that preteens were sensitive about being considered young. "How did you know Dylan was staying here?"

As if bored with the conversation, the girl looked around. "I wrote the address down from the papers he left with my mom."

Papers? Hmm. Maybe this wasn't simply a matter of a young fan stalking her hero. Why would Dylan deliver papers to her mom? Now Tessa was beyond curious. And she couldn't leave the girl outside forever while she figured it out. "Come on in and have a seat. Are you hungry? Thirsty? Can I get you something?"

"Nah. I'm good. I brought some Pop-Tarts in my bag," she said and tilted her head in the direction of her purple backpack, slung over one shoulder. She shuffled in, and Tessa shut the doors before following her over to the counter.

"Go ahead and hop up," Tessa said, pointing to the barstools.

Without argument, Elle climbed up. "So who are you? Dylan's girlfriend?"

Tessa nearly choked. No one had ever accused her of

being that. "No, definitely not. Just a former neighbor. He's actually best friends with my brother, Finn. We all kind of grew up together." Why was she babbling like this? The girl didn't need to know all these details. She cleared her throat. "What kind of papers did Dylan drop off with your mom?"

"She doesn't know I saw them, but I heard her talking about them last night on the phone to my Aunt Tristan. I guess he saw the test results and decided he wanted to give me and my mom some money."

Test results? It felt like someone had punched her in the gut. Was this girl...Dylan's? "You mentioned you were twelve, is that right?"

"Only for two more months."

That would mean Elle would have had to have been conceived just over thirteen years ago, back when Dylan was about...nineteen. His first year of college. Her hands shook as she grabbed a couple Dr. Peppers from the fridge, sliding one across the counter to her guest before popping open the other and talking a careful sip.

Tessa studied her more closely. The arc of freckles that fell cheek to cheek and the crooked front teeth were less familiar to Tessa, but the light brown eyes with specks of gold were familiar. As was that bravado.

Was this why Dylan was here? Because he'd found out he was...a dad?

Her knees were going to give out on her soon. After coming around the island, she slipped onto a barstool.

"I knew all along what the tests were going to say. I even tried to tell him when I went to see him at his concert, but he didn't want to believe me. I guess the test results did what I couldn't. So now he's all feeling guilty and wants to unload a lot of money on us, which has really ticked my mom off."

"Oh, sure. Sure," Tessa said and took another fortifying drink. Who was this woman? Had Dylan loved her? "It must have come as a shock for him to find out he had a daughter all this time."

"Daughter?" Elle asked and turned to stare at her like Tessa had grown another head. "Ew. Dylan isn't my dad. He's my brother."

Tessa blinked. Brother?

The relief that hit her was intense and she felt almost dizzy.

Dylan didn't have a kid out there—at least as far as they all knew. But he did have a sister.

That it mattered to Tessa that Dylan wasn't a dad was crazy. He could do what he wanted with who he wanted. And yet it did matter. For whatever reason.

It made sense now. Why Dylan might have taken some time off and come out here to the farm. Especially since Santa Rosa was only twenty minutes away.

Maybe the blood test results hadn't been that much of a surprise. Come to think of it, he had been a bit mellow after his visit with Jasper yesterday. That was probably the business he'd had to attend to.

"So Dylan sent you and your mom money and now she's mad," Tessa said, recounting the conversation now in a different light. "And you're here because..."

"I dunno," Elle said and slurped her soda. "I was kinda hoping that maybe he might want to, you know...hang out. Get to know me. Do what brothers and sisters do together. Do you have any brothers or sisters?"

"Five brothers. No sisters, though."

The girl's eyes widened. "Five brothers? You're so lucky. I bet you got to do all sorts of things together."

"We had our moments." Tessa thought about the Uber

driver who'd dropped the girl off. "I'm guessing that your mom doesn't know you're here."

Elle glanced up at her, the guilt in those light brown eyes telling Tessa the answer.

"Don't you think she's going to be upset with you when she finds out you came all the way out here without telling her?" Tessa asked.

"Maybe. But I knew if I asked, she would never let me come, and I really wanted to see Dylan. Besides, she thinks I'm at school," she whispered in a tone that seemed to indicate that the depth of her deception was starting to hit her—and the amount of trouble she was going to be in.

The girl was certainly brave, coming out here on her own. Brave and curious and determined, just like her brother, but also diving headfirst into trouble without thinking of the consequences.

She felt some sympathy for the girl's plight, could even understand why she'd done what she did in coming here. The least Tessa could do was make sure Elle had the opportunity to see the person who was the entire reason she was here since she'd probably be grounded forever.

"Let me text Dylan. He left pretty early this morning, so I'm not sure where he is right now. You're welcome to hang out with me until he gets here if you want. But in the meantime, let's call your mom and let her know you're here. The phone is over there," she said, pointing to the aging wireless receiver over on the counter that her dad refused to upgrade.

Elle's shoulders noticeably sagged. "It's okay. I have my own cell phone." She hopped down and dug in her backpack until she found the phone, an older, basic model, but it would do the job.

Tessa listened as the girl called, her voice wavering as

she spoke, growing quiet as her mom reamed into her, something that Tessa could hear bits and pieces of from her seat next to Elle. After another minute, Elle held the phone out to her. "My mom wants to talk to you."

Even though she wasn't in trouble, Tessa felt a tremor of anxiety as she answered. "Hi, this is Tessa."

"Yes. Hi. This is Lana, Elle's mom. I'm just— I'm at a loss here. I don't know what she was thinking. I'd come out there right now and get her if I didn't think I'd lose my job."

"Please, she's perfectly welcome to stay here with me. Like I told her, Dylan isn't here but I've texted him, so hopefully I should hear from him soon."

The woman didn't say anything immediately, and the seconds beat by before she spoke again. "Actually, he was here earlier. At the diner." She sighed, and Tessa imagined a woman torn between her responsibilities to her daughter and her job, knowing ultimately that, as long as her daughter was safe, it was best to protect her primary means of support. "I guess if you don't mind her hanging around, I'm okay with it. Well, I'm as okay with it as I can be under the circumstances. Can you have Dylan call me, however, when he gets there?"

"Of course. And let me give you our phone number here at the farm if you need to reach us directly." She listed the number, and after more assurances that Elle wouldn't be a bother, they ended the call.

Mission accomplished, she took Elle to the closet down the hall where twenty years' worth of games had been stashed. Elle stood and stared at the stacks of boxes, her face alight with excitement.

"Wow. You own all these?" she asked, studying the titles before grabbing two.

Tessa suppressed a groan when she saw that one of her

choices was Monopoly, the world's longest and most tedious games ever—and she should know having played it for years with her brothers. The other game, Rummikub, wasn't too bad. Just in case she couldn't talk Elle into abandoning Monopoly, Tessa grabbed the deck of cards from a shelf and escorted the girl back to the kitchen.

They were starting their second game of Rummikub when the kitchen door opened and Dylan waltzed in.

"So who is this mysterious guest who I—" He stopped when he spotted Elle.

Tessa supposed she could have prepared him for his moment by telling him exactly who his young guest was, but since he hadn't been exactly forthright with the fact he even had a sister and she'd nearly had a heart attack when she thought Elle was his daughter, Tessa figured she could stand to keep him in the dark for a few minutes.

"Elle. What are you— Wait. Please tell me that your mom knows you're here?"

Elle studied her tiles and muttered, "She does now."

"Don't worry. We called and let her know she was here," Tessa said. "I've assured her that Elle's safe here with me and that you would call her when you arrived."

He looked less than thrilled at the prospect of calling the mom, making her think today's meeting that Lana had mentioned hadn't gone very well. Dylan seemed to be thinking something over, his eyes on the floor as if processing. Another moment passed, and whatever he'd been wrestling with seemed to be decided as he walked over and took a chair between them.

"You know, we're going to have to work out a few things. You can't keep taking off like this, not just because your mom will kill us both, but because it's not safe." Something seemed to occur to him. "Shouldn't you be in school right now?"

Seeming to sense that Dylan had accepted her presence and wasn't mad, Elle's demeanor noticeably relaxed as she pulled her tiles from the bag and counted them out. "Today's a catch-up day for missing assignments and stuff, and since I'm already ahead, I would have just spent the day in the library anyhow."

"Still, you should have called first. Found a day and time that worked for everyone and that wouldn't have required you to skip school."

Elle looked down, her attention on moving the tiles around on her board. "I was afraid you would say no. That you didn't want to see me. Like before."

Tessa met his gaze, both of them feeling the pain in the girl's voice. She wanted to say something but knew that, right now, Dylan should have the floor.

"That's fair. After the way I treated you in LA, I could see why you'd think that. I'm sorry for how abrupt I was," Dylan continued. "You took me by surprise is all. By the next day, when I was thinking clearer, I did everything I could to find out what I could about you. In fact, I even paid a visit to your mom today to try and make things right."

"You did?" she asked.

"Sure did. Because I think that you and I probably have a lot in common and I'd like to know everything I can about my newfound sister."

The little girl glowed with pleasure at his words. "Does that mean I can hang out with you a little longer today? Maybe even stay for dinner?"

"Sorry, kid. But you know that what you did was wrong, and if I let you stay, I'd be rewarding that. Now, I'm going to give your mom a call and then I'm going to drive you back to

Santa Rosa. By my estimate"—he glanced at his watch —"you could be back at school in time for lunch."

"Really?" Elle asked, her face dropping in disappointment.

He met Tessa's gaze again and she tilted her head, as if pleading with him to give Elle a little something,

"Okay. We'll have lunch. But then you're going back to school. And if you want to come and see me again, you're going to do it the right way. By getting your mom's and my clearance. Got it?"

Elle sighed. "O-kay."

Wow. That was almost...mature. Tessa had to just take one look into those big brown eyes and she was ready to give the girl whatever she wanted, but Dylan was showing remarkable restraint and—

"Can we maybe play just one more game of Rummikub?"

He hesitated. "One more. Right after I call your mom."

Okay. So it was a work in progress.

It was close to eight that night when Dylan rolled up again to the farmhouse. After dropping off Elle earlier this afternoon, he'd been somewhat embarrassed to face Tessa, and instead of facing her again and being subjected to her inevitable questions, he'd gone over to his aunt's to discuss the situation.

But now he was ready.

Only walking into the house and chatting with Joe and Finn, he'd learned Tessa wasn't there. And suddenly, having spent the afternoon and evening avoiding her, he realized how much he wanted to talk to her. Her car was outside, so his guess was she was somewhere in walking distance.

When he stepped outside, there was still a little bit of that hazy light that afforded him an inspection of the surrounding grounds. The vineyards that covered half of the Montenegros' property and had been buzzing with frenetic energy just one week ago were strangely still and quiet, as were the orchards. No sign of Tessa to be found.

On a hunch, he made his way to the old holding pond, where, as kids, they'd all sneak away on hot summer nights for some fun and a little cooldown. And where once he'd been stupid enough to risk everything for one tiny kiss.

Sure enough, he found her sitting on the very same rock they'd sat on the night everything changed, staring pensively ahead.

"Wondered when you'd stop hiding from me," she said suddenly, not taking her gaze from the water.

He came over and took a seat next to her, picking up some rocks as he did so, throwing the first to skim across the water. "Not hiding. More...processing."

Tessa nodded, taking a rock from his hand and sending it across the water at least two feet farther than his. "She's a great kid. Smart and independent and with a bit of a stubborn streak like someone else I know. I bet you were surprised when she showed up that first time?"

"You could say that. As you can tell, I didn't handle myself that well with the bombshell, something I'm working to rectify."

"Is she why you're here? In Blossom Falls?"

He paused and glanced in her direction. The night was cooler, probably in the lower sixties, and, save for the black rubber boots on her feet, Tessa wasn't dressed very well for it in those cutoffs and the teensy formfitting T-shirt that had her gripping her knees up to her chest for warmth. He felt that familiar sort of protectiveness rise in his chest when it came to her, and he slid closer, as if to offer her some of his own body heat. "In part. But even before she arrived, I was needing to get away. I doubt you would have heard, but my dad passed in July."

She studied him, her brow furrowing. "I hadn't heard. I'm sorry, Dylan."

"No need. I'm not brokenhearted or anything. I'd written him off a long time ago," he said more cavalierly than he felt. "But I was in a weird place when Elle arrived. She just pushed me the rest of the way here."

Not that he'd known why at the time. He'd just known that the answers would be here. But the reason Blossom Falls was the answer was becoming clear.

This was home.

"Is that why I haven't seen you pick up a guitar since I arrived here? You know"—she glanced over to him, her green eyes holding a trace of concern along with curiosity —"I remember a time when it used to never leave your side, all those long mornings and evenings when you would just sit and strum the strings because you couldn't help it."

He could remember that, too. The evenings most notably, sitting on the porch at his aunt's house playing to the birds and sometimes Tessa Montenegro, who often found ways to be underfoot. She'd been his harshest critic but also his biggest fan.

"Do you remember the big bake sale you spearheaded to help out at the animal shelter that summer? You were probably not much older than Elle, and yet you managed to talk me into playing 'Hound Dog' and 'Teddy Bear.'"

She laughed. "Thanks to *Lilo and Stitch*, I had a bit of

an Elvis crush at the time. But to be fair, the songs were a big hit."

"Yes, they were," he said and chuckled. "It was actually my first paying gig. You gave me twenty dollars for my efforts."

"A high sum indeed that you were smart enough to donate back to the shelter."

"At threat of my life," he said and nudged her.

"All for a good cause."

True. As were all the missions she'd undertaken. He would have been fifteen years old at the time, and although the crowd was small, it had been the first time he'd actually performed outside of his lessons or for someone besides his aunt and the rest of the Montenegros.

It had lit the light in him, helped him realize the road he wanted to take, and sticking around the sleepy California town was never going to be it.

"You still haven't answered my question. About playing," she persisted, prodding him with her arm.

He scratched the back of his neck as he considered her question. "I'm sure the music will come to me with time." At least he hoped so.

She stared at him like she wasn't buying it, not that he could blame her, but saying it out loud sounded oddly true. "And what about you? What made you decide to pick up law of all things?"

"Maybe it was like that bake sale or the other fundraisers I've worked on over the years. Having a purpose, something to fight for, people—or animals—to help has always been fulfilling for me. Learning about the law seemed like the best way I could channel that energy and do some good, much like Jasper did."

"And that's what you're doing now? Finding reward in helping people?"

She squirmed and looked away. "Well, not exactly. Not yet. I've only been out of law school for three years, and at a big law firm like mine, there's a sort of dues that needs to be paid before you can stretch out into what you really want to do. So for now, it's a lot of contract work, a lot of real estate finagling and little else."

"You could go out on your own, though, right? Like Jasper?"

"Maybe. Someday."

He wondered if he was overstepping the boundaries of their new friendship by his next question, but he was curious. "Does it make you happy, though? What you're doing?"

"I don't know," she said, and sighed. "Does playing for the millions of devoted fans make you happy?"

He considered her question. "It did initially. Standing up there, the energy from the crowd surrounding me, the music flowing not just through my fingertips but from deep inside... It's a buzz and you feel incredibly alive. There's almost nothing quite like it. That carried me on for a while. Maybe too long, to be honest, as I did all the stupid, reckless things that people do when they get too popular too fast and have way too much money."

"I heard," she said, sounding somewhat disgruntled. "Like driving your new Ferrari into a fire hydrant when your passenger got a little too...affectionate?"

He grinned. That was putting it more mildly than he deserved. Even his agent had reamed him a new one, and his appearance at the next week's Grammy awards was almost put into jeopardy. But he'd made it through and, if anything, only earned more attention and sales from the stunt. Intentional or not.

"You're such a pig," she said as she caught his expression and punched him in the arm.

He shrugged good-naturedly.

"You said almost," she said suddenly. "What did you mean?"

He paused, racking his brain for what she was referring to.

"You said that you felt alive up there, performing for your fans. That there was almost nothing quite like it. Something must have exceeded that for you then. What was it?"

She was sometimes too astute for her own good. He tried to figure out how to explain it. "The only time I ever felt anything close to being onstage was back here. In Blossom Falls. Surrounded by Aunt Daphne, Finn, your entire family, actually." And her, he thought immediately but couldn't bring himself to admit out loud. "That feeling of being a part of something, connected, as we sat together at Thanksgiving dinner or on Christmas morning, sharing cake at everyone's birthday parties. Heck, even roasting marshmallows out at the fire pit as your dad told us those ghost stories that we all pretended not to be scared of until it was time to head to bed... Those moments, those feelings, they just can't be matched."

She nodded and her eyes sparkled with warmth and understanding. How could she not realize how beautiful she was? Her beauty was quiet and steadfast, not flashy like some of the actresses and supermodels he'd dated these past years.

Her beauty was innocent and fresh but infinitely sexier.

Made him think of taking her hand in his, feeling the connection that he'd always fought against but that now seemed to beckon him. Of being able to tickle her under the ribs, like when they were kids, until she squealed for him to stop, which he would do this time but only after bringing her up close against him and settling into the soft curves and valleys of that pint-sized frame.

Of tilting her head, inhaling everything about her before he leaned in to kiss her.

As if he was meant to.

———

TESSA FOUND herself wanting to swim in the depths of Dylan's eyes as he studied her, a strange light entering them that had her breath catching in her throat.

What was he thinking about? What secrets lay behind that grin?

She couldn't take the suspense, the energy that crackled in the few inches that separated them, and she came to her feet quickly. "It's getting colder out here than I expected. I'm going to head back while I can still feel my fingers and toes."

He rose slowly and took a step toward her, closing the space between them.

Too close. She needed to get away and she stepped back, needing the distance.

A bad move since, so distracted, she hadn't realized how close she was to the edge, and in the next moment, she was falling backwards. Dylan's hand swept out to grab her, but instead of finding purchase, his face widened in surprise as he fumbled forward, both of them falling down into the cold, murky water of the pond.

The cold water hit her hard. Through elbows and knees and the heavy hulk on top of her, she found the surface and gasped for breath. The water was deeper here, which was why it had always been the favored spot for jumping, and right now she was struggling from her boots and the onslaught of water in her lungs to stay afloat. As if he sensed her peril, a strong, steady arm was around her waist and she clung to it, accepting its warmth and stability as he pulled her to shallower water, where he seemed to have found footing. With her other hand, she pushed a mop of wet hair from her eyes and the grass and sludge from her face.

It was then the humor of the situation hit her, and she burst out laughing, a sentiment that Dylan echoed with a gust of his own laughter that rocked his chest—and her—as he did. "I've heard girls say how they'd fallen for me and all, but never before have I actually seen it."

"You wish," she said, splashing him, a gesture he easily dodged.

He took a moment to shove back a strand of his own hair that was hanging over his face before settling his hand on her hip. His touch felt like a brand, and she flinched.

"Hey. Remember that summer when you were obsessed with that movie? *Dirty Dancing*?" he asked, unaware of the effect his hand was having on her.

Of course she remembered. She'd watched the movie every night, rewinding it to her favorite parts, insisting that every single Montenegro brother—and Dylan—watched it at least three times. She shrugged. "Vaguely."

"Vaguely? You'd think the fact you nearly drowned me trying to recreate the lift scene in this very spot would have etched a more lasting memory."

She laughed. "Okay, fine. I wanted to live in that movie, I loved it so much."

"We were actually pretty good. Once we got the hang of it."

She remembered it all and how no amount of pleading

and begging could convince her brothers to undertake the move, but how Dylan had ultimately relented, always her hero.

He smiled more devilishly. "Want to give it a try?"

"Try?" She blinked. "You want to try and lift me now? I was fourteen last time we did that, when I had no fear of falling. Unlike now," she said, suddenly nervous at the prospect of his hands on *both* of her hips.

"Is there something better you have to do? Come on. It will be fun."

Okay. So his suggestion was utterly ridiculous. She was beyond that obsession, and yet...

She eyed his arms, bulging underneath his tee shirt that now clung to his body, every nuance outlined in the moonlight.

Man. She really wanted to do it.

"All right. One time. But you're going to have to take me somewhere I can actually push off."

Without another word, he stepped back until she could find her footing. One thing was certain. She was going to have to lose the boots. The silt of the pond sucked at her feet every step she took, making her feel like the swamp creature as she walked to the pond's edge, where she pulled them off and tossed them aside. She pulled her shirt down, wondering if she was really about to do this.

"Okay. You asked for it."

She stepped slowly, making sure her foot didn't hit anything alive and squishy, until she was only a few feet away from him. He nodded, letting her know her cue, and, taking a deep breath, she pushed off with her feet to get a semi-running start before leaping up. Only her jump wasn't as graceful as she'd have liked from the yelp below her as her elbow smacked him on the head.

She laughed despite herself. "Sorry. I warned you."

He rubbed his head. "Let's try it again."

Three tries later, they hadn't been any more successful. At a mere fourteen, Tessa was practically fearless. She'd put her mind to doing that jump, and she'd done it. Right now, however, Tessa was struggling to let herself feel that fearlessness.

But she'd give it another go. One more breath in and she ran, plunging forward as she told herself that there was nothing to fear. Strong arms and warm hands were under her, helping to push her up until she was breaking the surface of the water and almost flying.

She was doing it. She was really doing it.

A sentiment that lasted another two seconds when she looked down and saw the light in Dylan's eyes as he held her. It looked almost like...attraction? Desire? Admiration?

Was he looking up her shirt?

Immediately, she lost her balance and fell, his arms there to hold on to her as she plunged under the water again. Sputtering from the mouthful of water, she coughed and let herself be held in his arms.

"You okay?" he asked.

She nodded. "I guess maybe some things can't be repeated."

It was then she recognized how easily her body seemed to fit against his, her legs sliding around each of his hips as she rested her weight on him so they faced each other. His body was a beacon of heat compared to the coldness of the water, and she drew nearer as did he, their breathing loud in her ears as she watched the water dripping down his face, over the fine blond hair of his beard, and down his neck. His throat convulsed and she raised her gaze to meet his.

She almost didn't see his kiss coming, the bow of his

head as he tipped it so his lips could slide across hers, barely a whisper at first, his breath against her skin. Then he was gone, leaning back as he studied her reaction.

When she blinked and lifted her mouth higher, he seemed to understand what she wanted as his lips found hers again, stronger now against hers, urging her mouth to open to him. And she did, gripping his shoulders as she brought him even closer.

This was what she'd been resisting the moment she saw him. This attraction, this energy that always existed between them, drawing them closer. For that moment, she let her eyes close, let him in through the barrier she'd built around herself. This was what it was like to love and be—

She froze as she realized what she was thinking.

No. This couldn't happen. Not again. She wouldn't let herself feel that pain again when he left.

"Stop," she said and pushed away from his warmth and solidness. But this time she was closer to the shallow end, and in a few strokes, she was standing on her own, backing away from him. "This can't happen."

The sucking ground of the pond slowed her progress until she reached the edge, where she snatched her boots and glanced back.

Dylan's exit was slower, his grin so deep that she could almost see his dimples even through the thickness of that beard. His slow steps that continued in her direction had the bells going off in her head again, but in an unfortunate stroke of luck, the bells seemed to have conflicting messages.

On one hand, she was flooded with foreboding that had her ready to run without looking back. On the other, she had to fight the urge to jump back in his arms and see exactly where that kiss might lead.

Fortunately, sense and self-preservation seemed to win

out, and she managed to keep her footing as, boots clutched in her hand, she walked barefoot away from him and in the direction of the farmhouse.

"Good night, Tessa," Dylan called out seconds later, his voice farther behind, telling her he wasn't following. Which was a relief.

Wasn't it?

Reaching the sanctuary of the porch, she dropped her boots and pushed the back door open, relieved that no one was around to see her. She was aware of the water trail she left behind her, but she could clean that up later, and she continued up the stairs and into the bathroom, where she shut the door and locked it.

She leaned against the door, her legs wobbly and numb.

What the heck had just happened? How could she have let that happen? Hadn't she learned her lesson before? Was she completely insane?

When she was sure her feet wouldn't give out from under her, she went over and started the shower, eager to get the pond scum and slime off of her. But as she stood under the spray of the water, it was hard not to remember the feeling of his body under hers. His lips, his mouth, his hands—

Crap.

She was in trouble.

SEVEN

Tessa found an empty parking spot in the parking lot of Cooper's Market and pulled in.

"Hold on, Dad. I'll help you out," she said, unbuckling her seat belt and opening her door.

"I'm perfectly capable of opening a door, thank you very much."

Tessa sighed and grabbed her purse before climbing out. Men.

It was just past noon on Wednesday, sixteen hours since Dylan had planted that kiss on her, leaving her tense and anxious and jumping out of her skin all morning at every sound, horrified that she was about to come face-to-face with the guy who'd brought back those feelings she'd thought she'd left in the past.

But her anxiety had been for nothing as Dylan had already left early that morning, and he'd still been AWOL by the time she and her dad left the house.

Distraction and avoidance. That's what she needed to get through the next few days of living in the same house as the devil before she could return to her normal, predictable life. Which was why, instead of waiting for the moment she was confronted with Dylan, she'd decided she and her dad needed to get out.

Not surprisingly, her dad had given her no argument, since he'd been feeling restless himself the past few days.

Her dad seemed to be as lost in his thoughts as she was in hers as they shopped, their footfalls slow and measured as they went down the aisles, Tessa careful to keep her pace even with his.

"I think the only thing left on the list is laundry soap," she said twenty minutes later as they reached that aisle.

"Here," her dad said, reaching for the large box of their usual soap.

"Whoa, whoa, whoa. Not so fast," she said, leaping forward to stop him. "You're not supposed to be lifting or carrying that much. Let me get this, Dad."

He didn't argue but he did mutter something under his breath that she figured was probably better she didn't understand. Her arms were full of the twenty-five pound box when her phone rang from the grocery cart, where she'd left it resting on top of her purse.

Tessa grunted as she squatted down to shove the soap under the cart and stood up, reaching for the phone, noticing her dad had leaned over to scan the caller ID.

She nearly jumped back when she saw Eric's name flashing as it rang.

Thank heavens she'd seen the name before she picked up. She hadn't heard from him since Saturday night when she'd ended things, and she was surprised that, after what she said, he was still reaching out.

"You going to get that?" her dad asked as she stood there.

"Nah. It can wait." The phone finally stilled and the screen darkened. "Anything else you can think of we need?"

"Think we've got it all," he said more thoughtfully as he stared at her before moving ahead to the checkout.

They were standing in the line a minute later when Jan Huckleberry joined them, her youngest granddaughter, who could be no more than four years old, in tow.

"Look at you, Joe Montenegro," Jan said in an overly concerned tone. "What on earth are you doing up and about like this? You should be off your feet and at home resting." She directed her stern gaze in Tessa's direction, however, as she shook her head in disapproval. "I can't tell you how worried I've been thinking about you out there alone on that farm these past few days, and if I didn't have my grandkids with me seeing as how my daughter is on vacation, I would have stopped by."

"Thanks for your concern, Jan, but Tessa here's been home with me since Sunday and she's been taking good care of me. Believe me, I'm here at the doctor's recommendation. She's told me that I can get out and make some use of this new hip. What are you up to, Jemima?" he asked, leaning down to greet the little girl, his effort showing as he gritted his teeth.

"Nan said if I'm good we'll see the puppies," she chirped.

"Puppies, huh?" he asked.

"They had a whole new litter over at the animal shelter that we thought we'd stop by and take a look at," Jan explained. She paused as if something struck her. "Did you want to join us? That is, if you don't think you'd be over-doing it?"

Tessa waited for her dad to make the usual excuse that it was probably best that he get on his way, but to her shock, he nodded. "I think that sounds like fun. I know Tessa probably has another errand or two she'd like to take care of without my holding her back."

Something she couldn't deny, but she felt like she should be objecting all the same. Leaving him with Jan Huckleberry, whose husband had died a few years back and, as consolation, had immersed herself, almost obsessively, in her kids' and now her grandkids' lives? She could hardly have anything to talk about with him.

"Are you sure? I was just driving over to Claudia's place to say hello and see how she's taking the news of the closure of her art studio." And to see if she might convince the woman that maybe all wasn't lost and Tessa could help her fight it if she wanted to. "I shouldn't be that long."

"You dad will be just fine with us, dear," Jan said, smiling, a little too pleased. "All we'll be doing is playing with the puppies and getting an ice cream cone."

Tess waited for her dad's usual attitude to appear that would tell Jan she didn't have a chance with him. But instead he smiled fondly at the woman, his blue eyes warm and friendly. Tessa gulped. "Whatever you want to do, Dad."

"I don't think an ice cream cone could hurt anyone. You can text me when you're all done."

The young kid behind the checkout finished ringing up their items, and Tessa ran her credit card through the machine, taking two tries before she finally got it right, her mind numb. Grabbing the bags in one arm and the detergent in the other, she returned her attention to her dad.

"Okay. I guess I'll see you in about an hour. Call me if you need me, okay?"

"Sure, honey. You go on and enjoy yourself."

Yeah, you, too, Dad, she wanted to say with a less-than-enthused tone, but settled for a nod as she hurried to the car. Maybe the fresh air and new scenery after being so cooped up at home had given him a temporary delirium? That could be the only reason he'd take Jan up on her offer to hang out with them.

After piling the groceries inside the car, she drove to her next destination. Claudia Nunn's.

Her research had turned up a couple of cases, and she was going to at least share what she learned with Claudia. It was a bittersweet sight as she pulled up and parked in the small lot that lined the fence between Claudia's house and art studio. She read the sign in front.

Thank you, Blossom Falls, for allowing me to paint with you these past forty-two years.

Forty-two years. That was more than Tessa had realized. It might actually help implement her plan.

The door of the studio was open, and she could hear music playing softly from inside, drawing her in. As she suspected, despite this probably being the studio's last week, Claudia was walking around the back of the studio, offering encouragement and tips to the five students painting. Ranging in age from seventy to ninety, the senior group was immersed in the art on the easels before them and hadn't noticed her arrival.

Claudia saw her, though, and waved. "Tessa Montenegro. So good to see you. What can I help you with?"

Even after all these years, Claudia looked just as Tessa remembered. Her gray hair cut short so—as she used to put it—she didn't have to keep brushing it back and could focus on the art, her blue eyes merry and filled with warmth and understanding.

"Oh, I only wanted to stop and say hello," Tessa said, "but I can come back later when you're not busy."

"My class has five more minutes if you want to wait. Explore the room until then."

"Great. I think I will."

Walking around the room, Tessa smiled at the art and photos that covered most of the walls. She nearly choked when she caught sight of a painting of her own. A brightly painted picture of her mom's flower garden, and even though Tessa's skills were pretty basic, she could make out the gladiolas and the poppies, the violets and the rose bushes that once filled the garden so vibrantly. She would guess that she'd probably been around seven when she did this one.

She didn't know how long she stood staring at the image when she felt Claudia reach her side. "I'm all yours, m'dear," she said cheerily.

Tessa looked around, surprised to see everyone had already cleared out. Claudia was still studying Tessa's painting. "Even back then I could see your talent."

Tessa looked at her like she was crazy. "This isn't even very good."

"Art is about the expression of emotions and you did that beautifully."

Tessa smiled. "You always did know what to say. I can't quite wrap my head around the fact that you're going to be closing after all these years. You taught me so much."

"Thank you. I will be sorry to see the place close down, but all things must end eventually."

Now was her chance. "That's what I wanted to speak to you about. Did Jasper tell you I was looking into the gas company's claim?"

"He mentioned something."

"I've been doing some research, and I think if we can get enough attention on what's happening through the local television stations and papers, maybe even a spot in the *LA Times*—"

"I don't want you to go to any trouble, Tessa."

"But it wouldn't be any trouble. My friend writes for the *Times* and I know she'll be happy to help get some attention on this. With the right pressure and negative publicity, we could get the gas company to deviate from their plans. I mean, forty-two years. It's practically an institution to Blossom Falls, you *and* this place."

Claudia patted her arm, her eyes sympathetic. "I understand how much this place meant to you, Tessa, and it brings me pleasure to know that you'd be willing to do all of that for me. But I don't want to fight this. True, it took me by surprise, and Lord knows how much this place has meant to me over the years. But I'm seventy-four years old, and as much as I love this, I'm getting weary. I have a daughter who lives in San Diego, who's been wanting me to come and move closer to her and my grandkids, and with this opportunity, the money...well, I could sell the place for a tidy sum and find something closer to her and still have a fair amount to keep me afloat."

The list of reasons, of case names and plans that Tessa had been working on suddenly were forgotten, and she took a moment to try and grasp what was happening.

Claudia really was okay with this. Better than okay. She was probably going to end up with a nice sum that would set her up for the rest of her life.

How could she argue with that? Yes, the community might still need an art studio, but this was no longer Claudia's burden and she couldn't make it seem like it was.

"I see," Tessa said, feeling deflated. "So you're really okay with this?"

"I really am, and as much as I'm sad for the community, the town is growing so much and thriving such that my little studio will hardly be missed."

"That's not true. And if it is, then I don't accept that. Growing up, I found this place such a sanctuary, and I'm sure that it's helped so many others over the years that it would be a tragedy that it all has to come to an end."

"It's just a shame you live so far away, dear. I'm sure with your drive and energy, you could have come up with some solutions for the community. Let's hope that someone else sees the value in this place and what it provided and they'll find a way to continue it."

Tessa wasn't so sure, having a sinking feeling that, once Claudia left, so would this small piece of Blossom Falls, and it broke her heart.

"In the meantime," Claudia continued, "the Ladies' Guild is throwing me a big farewell party next Saturday in the town square. I hope you'll be able to make it."

"I wish I could but I'll be back in the city by then."

"Come on. Don't look so dreary," Claudia said and smiled. "I was going to make myself some tea. Try and read a little of this book that we're scheduled to discuss at this evening's book club. But I'm afraid at this late date I won't get much read. Maybe you could join me for tea instead?"

Tessa looked around at the open, airy room, knowing that it was probably the last time she would see it. But she was up in arms to fight a battle that no one saw the value of but her. Maybe Claudia was right. Someone would take it up. Maybe, someday.

In the meantime, she could say one last good-bye to another memory of her childhood.

Besides, it's not like her dad was waiting for her. He was busy playing with puppies and eating ice cream.

And Dylan...well, he was doing whatever it was he did. It made no difference to her. There was no rush, no need to race away to build a save-the-studio plan.

She returned Claudia's smile. "Tea sounds wonderful."

EIGHT

Dylan walked around the grounds of the old Wallace place, still stunned at the momentous decision he was considering. Ever since Jasper called him this morning to say that the current owner wasn't interested in selling off pieces of the property but would consider selling it all if the price were right, Dylan had been mulling over his options and coming to one conclusion.

He wanted the Wallace property. He wanted the land, the house, all the promise and potential that settling right here in Blossom Falls brought. Which was insanity considering that, for his entire life, the last thing he thought he wanted was to plant roots down anywhere. Hitting the road, finding places to travel, new crowds to play to had been the only things he wanted. Or thought he wanted.

Yet he'd done all that and he hadn't found any more peace or happiness than before he left Blossom Falls. If anything, quite the opposite.

But this? Buying this property, making it his? This felt right. Just like a lot of things that had been happening since he arrived.

Like that kiss. When he'd set out to find Tessa, he hadn't any intention of doing what he'd done. But kissing her had been the most natural thing he'd done in a long time, and he didn't regret it.

He looked over to his aunt, who had just finished circling the front of the house. "The bones of the old place seem solid. You could do a lot worse. And I'm not just saying that because I would love nothing more than to have you five minutes away from me again."

"Of course you're not," he teased. He studied the front of the two-story structure that had once been painted white but had dulled to gray over the decades, the wide, inviting porch that—if his foot going through the wood was any indication—had started to rot, and the windows that had been broken and the hinges loose. But he didn't really see problems, only potential.

"What are you going to do?" she prodded him.

"I'll take a day or two just to be sure I haven't lost my mind. If I'm still wanting it, I'll have Jasper reach out with an offer." He checked his watch. "I should get going. Did you want to head over to the farmhouse with me? Say hello?"

She looked away. "Nah. I have a roasted chicken in the oven at home. But tell everyone I said hello."

He wanted to ask her if her sudden avoidance of the farm had anything to do with the news that Joe Montenegro had been seen having ice cream with Jan Huckleberry yesterday, but it wasn't his business, and he doubted she'd say anything even if he asked.

"All right. I'll see you later," he said and hugged her before getting into the truck and driving to the farmhouse, the thought of seeing Tessa again bringing a smile to his face.

A half-dozen cars were parked in the drive, none of which he recognized. Curious, he headed inside, where the kitchen was empty but the sound of voices and laughter, high and definitely feminine, coming from the other room, told him where the party was located.

"Good evening," he said uncertainly as he stepped in the room and found nearly every seat taken by bright, eagerly smiling women of various ages, whose attention was now decidedly on him. He gulped, looking for a familiar face.

Tessa sat in the middle of the couch, a sly, satisfied expression on her face, likely at the look of bewilderment on his own. "Why, Dylan. We're so glad you could join us," she said. "You remember Claudia?"

He looked to her right, recognizing the older woman. "Course I do. Hi, Claudia."

"Dylan, I hope you don't mind the intrusion," Claudia said. "But we had a last-minute cancellation at the bookstore where we were supposed to have our book club meeting, and Tessa was kind enough to offer up the farm."

What a happy coincidence. Here he was looking forward to a little alone time with Tessa, maybe even getting a repeat of the kiss from the night before, and she was hosting half the town in the front room.

"You should stay, Dylan," a blond woman said from the rocking chair in the corner. "We'd love a man's perspective on things."

Stay? In a room full of women all looking at him like he was the last piece of chocolate cake? "I'm afraid I wouldn't be of much help on that—"

"Please, Dylan. We insist," Tessa said with a mischievous glint in her eye. "Dad's joining us, too, if you're worried you'll be outnumbered."

"I'm coming, I'm coming," the older Montenegro said from down the hall at that moment. After entering the room, he eased onto the La-Z-Boy recliner that had been left open for him. A couple of women offered to help him down, fluffing pillows around him as they did, which, instead of fussing he was capable of seating himself as Dylan expected him to say, Joe only smiled and thanked them.

From Tessa's expression, she wasn't any less surprised than him.

"All right. I guess I can stay for a moment." Even if only for the entertainment factor.

IT WAS NEARLY midnight when Dylan heard the bedroom door three rooms away slowly creak open and the faint but unmistakable sound of footsteps creaking down the hall and to the stairs. His plan to appear to have gone to bed seemed to have done the trick.

He just had to give Tessa a few more minutes to get into her secret treat stash before he sprung his appearance on her, since the entire night, she'd done her best to avoid any alone time with him.

Quietly he pulled on a shirt and jeans, careful as he crept down the hall and down the stairs. As he'd suspected, she was sitting at the bar with a mug of tea in her hands and pile of cookies in front of her. She had one such cookie midair when he stepped inside the room.

"I knew you were holding out on me. Where have you been keeping those treasures?" he asked, enjoying the horror that filled her face as she realized she was busted.

Okay, maybe not so much enjoying it since there were better reactions he'd hoped to invoke in the woman.

Tessa bit into the cookie, glancing nervously around the room as if looking for an excuse to make an unexpected exit. "What makes you think I was hiding these?"

"Because I know that growing up with five brothers in the house taught you a thing or two about stashing the good stuff."

She didn't deny it, instead taking another bite that she chased with a mouthful of tea.

"You going to share?" he asked, nodding toward the cookies.

Reluctantly she took two from her pile and slid them his way. Dylan considered taking the seat next to her but then opted to remain standing opposite her so as to be able to study her better.

"It was an interesting night, wouldn't you say?" he asked.

"It was fine. Dad seemed to really enjoy himself," she added begrudgingly.

"Is that a bad thing?"

"Not at all," she said in a tone that told him it definitely was. "But after all these years of having no interest in the women who pushed themselves at him, it's a bit shocking to see this about-face. Did you know he's actually going on a date tomorrow night? With Tansy Mortensen, no less."

"Tansy? Which one was she?"

"The redhead who kept cooing every time he said something."

He managed not to laugh, knowing exactly who she meant. "I take it you're not particularly happy about this? You know, it's been ten years since your mom died," he said in a softer tone. "It was bound to happen."

"You don't think I know that?" she asked. "Of course he was bound to date. I just want to be sure he's doing it for the right reasons. Why now, when, for the past ten years, he's been fine with how things were? I mean, what if the accident caused some sort of brain hemorrhage?"

He smiled. "I'm sure he's fine. If anything, I think this accident made him face a lot of realities. Made him take stock of things, maybe realize that his life has been kind of lonely these past few years. With you guys all growing up and moving on with your own lives, it's only bound to get lonelier."

She took another sip of tea, as if mulling his words. Her hair was pulled up with a headband of some kind, and her face, even absent makeup, was glowing and radiant. He was getting other ideas, ideas about what she might do if he tried to kiss her again.

She glanced up from her cup, almost as if sensing his thoughts. Her green eyes widened as if she confirmed her suspicions. She cleared her throat and set her cup down, faking a yawn. "Well, it's pretty late. I think I'm going to turn in."

He shook his head, letting her know his disappointment. "Chicken."

She froze. "Chicken? I don't know what you're talking about."

He leaned forward, resting on his elbows. "You're chicken because you spent the entire evening doing your best to avoid me. And thereby avoided talking about what happened last night."

"Avoiding you?" She forced a laugh. "You're a bit full of yourself."

"Isn't that why you decided to invite half the female

population here tonight for a book club meeting when you haven't even read the book?"

"How would you know if I've read it or not?"

He raised a brow. "Have you?"

"That's beside the point. I doubt that half the people here tonight read it, either. Most of them only come to these things for the wine and the company."

"You didn't invite them here to avoid me?"

"I said that already. I invited them here because they wouldn't have had anywhere else to meet otherwise."

"Very generous. I was thinking you were worried that maybe you would find yourself unable to resist my charms again."

She scowled. "Oh, I can resist them, all right. Sorry to tell you but you're not as irresistible as you think."

"Is that right? Maybe you should give me another chance to find out. Just to be sure."

She jumped up, moving another foot back. "Nice try, but not going to happen."

"Are you telling me you didn't enjoy that kiss, because I sure as hell did and haven't thought about much else since."

"Is that why you disappeared like you did the entire day?"

Was that what she thought? Avoiding her was the last thing he'd been doing today. "My absence had nothing to do with avoiding you. I promise." He grinned as another thought occurred to him. "Are you saying that you missed me?"

"Like a dog misses fleas."

"Are you the dog in this analogy or am I?" he teased, coming round the counter, enjoying the flush on her cheeks that seemed to heighten the closer he got.

"Oh, no, you don't," she said. "Don't go getting any

more ideas about kissing me, Dylan Jamison. That kiss was a mistake and it's not one I plan on repeating."

"You didn't like it?" He took another step forward. "Because I got the distinct impression that you were enjoying it as much as I was."

"That's beside the point. I'm leaving in a few days, and eventually you'll be leaving, too. There's no need to complicate things any more than they already are."

"I like complications."

"I bet you do. But I don't. My life is perfectly complication-free right now, and that's precisely how it's going to stay. Now, before you do something you're going to regret—"

"Oh, I definitely wouldn't regret it."

But she continued as if she hadn't heard him. "—I'm heading to bed, and when I see you tomorrow, we're both going to pretend that nothing happened. Got it?"

She could pretend all she wanted but he'd seen the flash of passion in her eyes a moment ago, the same flash that she'd had when he kissed her the night before—and she kissed him back. And he was determined that he'd see that again, and soon.

But instead, he simply said, "Whatever you say, Tessa."

She looked like she had been ready to argue, but thrown off by his compliance, she opened her mouth and shut it again. "All right. Good night."

"Sweet dreams."

Without another word, she whirled around and scurried out, leaving him smiling as she did.

Because if he were any other man and she were another person, he might have conceded defeat. But they weren't. He'd known Tessa Montenegro since she was nine years old, and he knew when she was lying, and she had been lying, all right.

She knew this wasn't over. So did he.

And although he didn't yet know how Tessa fit in the grand scheme of what he saw for his life, he was willing to find out.

TESSA ROUNDED the corner of the road Friday evening, her ire and frustration no less now than it had been when she first set out on this walk an hour ago in an effort to gain clarity.

For a guy who had been turning on the charm as thick and heavy as he had the other night—telling her how much he wanted to kiss her and that he hadn't been avoiding her— Dylan had done a remarkable job making himself scarce over the next twenty-four hours.

Okay. So maybe she was as much mad and disappointed in him as she was in herself because, try as she might, she still hadn't been able to stop thinking about that kiss and how much she wanted more. Not just of kisses, but of Dylan's time, his energy, his conversation.

How was it that even after all this time, spending any kind of time with the guy made her feel more alive and happier than she'd been in a long time? Which was probably why, when she woke up yesterday, her thoughts had immediately gone to Dylan and she'd had a rush of strange excitement at seeing him again, despite all her assertions to the contrary.

Coming downstairs and discovering that he and Finn had left earlier to drive to Petaluma to talk with some suppliers and wouldn't be back until the next day had left her more disappointed than she had any right to feel. Mostly because she would have to sit on all these conflicting emotions without anyone to vent her frustration on, which only made her more furious.

Ahead of her, she caught sight of Finn's Jeep parked in his usual spot and her stomach fluttered. They were back.

She swallowed a moment of trepidation as she stood outside the door of the kitchen. He couldn't see how much his absence had impacted her.

The sound of laughter inside puzzled her as she tried to recognize it. Giving up, she opened the door and stepped inside, almost not quite believing the scene before her.

Elle was standing on a stool over at the island, Tessa's old apron wrapped around her as she mixed something in a large bowl in front of her. More bewildering was the figure next to her, wearing her mom's old apron as he attempted to crack an egg into another bowl. They both looked up to see her and smiled. The same smile.

Something fluttered again low in her belly as she took in their faces, not to mention the mess between the two of them.

"Hi, Tessa!" Elle chirped happily.

"Hey, Elle," Tessa said and came to the other side of the counter to see them better. "What are you guys up to?"

"Dylan and I are making chocolate chip cookies together. But I don't think Dylan's very good."

"I can see that," she said, smiling as she spotted more egg on the outside of the bowl than inside, along with a lot of white shells.

"A little appreciation, please, ladies," Dylan said, seeming to take their criticism in stride. Using a fork, he worked on digging the eggshell fragments from the bowl, but after a minute of getting nowhere, he put the fork down.

Picking up the bowl, he slid the contents in with the rest of the ingredients. "It adds protein," he added and winked at them both.

"Sure. Protein," Tessa said, unable to stop returning his smile.

Holy Josephine.

With his blond hair swooping down over his brow despite his attempt to push it away with the back of his hand, his brown eyes flecked with gold that were studying her now with interest, and that sly grin on his face, it was hard not to appreciate how good he looked.

Apron or not, he exuded sexy masculinity.

"Do you want to help?" Elle asked.

"Oh. I don't know," Tessa said, pulling her gaze from Dylan's. "I should check my work email and make sure my dad doesn't need anything."

"I'm sure your mail can wait, considering it is Friday evening," Dylan said. "And last I checked, your dad was just fine. Getting ready for his date."

Right. How could she forget? "I'm guessing your mom knows you're here this time, right?" she asked Elle.

"Yep. Not only that, but because she has to work a double tonight, she's letting me sleep over."

"A sleepover? Really?" she asked, glancing over to Dylan.

"I'm afraid so. She's stuck with me. Your dad said she could take Aidan's room, which means she'll be as far away from my snoring as possible."

Elle giggled. "I guess we're going to be next door to each other," she said and glanced shyly at Tessa. "But I don't snore. You don't have to worry."

The shuffling of steps outside the kitchen drew Tessa's gaze to the doorway as her dad appeared freshly shaven, his hair still damp and slicked back, and his best pressed blue shirt tucked into jeans. Her stomach sank. He definitely was going all out for tonight's date.

Dylan let out a low whistle. "Looking good, Joe. Who did you say you were going out with?"

"Tansy Mortensen," Tessa muttered.

Dylan nodded. "Solid choice there. So you're saying we shouldn't wait up for you?"

What exactly was Dylan implying? That her dad would spend the night with some woman on his first date? She glared at him, but he wasn't looking at her.

The front doorbell rang. "Looks like she's here," her dad said, suddenly looking a little paler than he had all day.

"Dad, are you sure you're okay? You know, if you're not feeling up to it, I could go tell her that you'll have to postpone it for another night." *Or never.* "You just had hip surgery. I'm sure she would understand."

"No, no. I'll be fine. Nothing to worry about." He patted Tessa on the arm, smiling reassuringly. "You all have a good night now and don't worry about me."

She watched him walk out and listened as he opened the door for his guest.

"Did you tell Tessa what was on tonight's agenda?" Dylan asked Elle, even though they both knew she hadn't.

"After we make cookies, we're ordering pizza from Mama Leoni's, which Dylan said is the best pizza in the entire state. Then we're going to play some games, and after, we're having a movie night. And then tomorrow we're going to the festival."

"Wow. That's quite the itinerary you've got there," Tessa said, trying to focus on Elle and not her dad, who, from the sound of it, had just closed the car door.

"I know. Ever since my mom said I could come yesterday, I've been working on all the things I wanted to do this weekend with you and Dylan."

Tessa paused. "Me *and* Dylan?"

"Yup. You did tell me last time that you'd show me how to play Speed, right? Wasn't that what it's called?"

"Yeah, that's what it's called." Tessa glanced over to Dylan, who was grinning from ear to ear, not even trying to hide his satisfaction. It was as if he'd planned this. Known that bringing Elle over would mean she'd have to interact with him despite her request to the contrary.

She didn't really see much choice now, did she?

"I would love nothing more than to hang out with you. So, what's the movie on tonight's agenda?" she asked, popping a chocolate chip into her mouth.

"*Dirty Dancing*. Don't worry, my mom already said we could watch it as long as Dylan forwards through all the gross stuff."

Dirty Dancing?

She glanced over at him again. He winked.

Oh. He was good.

IT WAS JUST after ten and Tessa was in the kitchen drizzling a gallon of butter on their second bowl of popcorn when she saw the headlights of a car turn into their drive and stop.

Dad was back. And earlier than she expected. She squinted as she tried to make out the occupants sitting inside.

She shouldn't be spying like this. She would only see something she couldn't unsee. Turning around, she returned to the island and grabbed the salt shaker and doused the popcorn liberally before grabbing the vanilla ice cream from the freezer.

She was pouring the sweet soda over three tall glasses filled with ice cream when she heard the back door jiggle, and a moment later, her dad came inside.

She tried to act surprised to see him. "Hey, Dad. You're back early. How did it go?"

"Fine, pumpkin." He came over and watched as she continued pouring, the foam rising precariously close to the top of the last glass. "Tansy sure likes to talk, though. I'm afraid I'm not used to so much conversation, what with living with the boys for so long. Frankly, it wore me out."

She smiled, pleased for admittedly selfish reasons that her dad wasn't as taken with Tansy as she evidently had been with him. "Well, we're all about to watch *Dirty Dancing* in the other room if you want to join us. I can make you a root beer float. I think we have some cream soda if you prefer that over the root beer."

He patted her shoulder. "I think I'm just going to turn in. You go enjoy yourself and I'll see you in the morning."

"Good night, Dad," she said, kissing him on his cheek before watching him lumber away.

Guilt hit her as she watched him go, suddenly seeming older and more alone than he had before. Sure, it was tough seeing him flirt and talk about dating women when she'd only ever seen him act like that with her mom. But if that's what he wanted, what he needed, she had to let go of this sadness. Had to be happy for him.

"You okay?" Dylan asked from the doorway.

"Just saying good night to Dad. He went to his room."

Dylan nodded. "I heard."

She met his gaze, noticing the sympathy in the depths of those brown eyes, eyes that didn't miss a thing.

"He's going to be okay, you know."

She nodded. "I know. It's just going to take me a little time to get used to it."

From the other room, the opening song to the movie began playing and Elle called out, "It's starting. Are you guys coming?"

Dylan moved forward and scooped up two of the glasses. "Guess we should probably get in there."

She smiled, suddenly glad that Dylan was here with her, as he seemed to be for any momentous events in her life.

"I wouldn't miss it."

NINE

Dylan was sitting outside on the porch early the next morning, his guitar in hand and a mug of coffee next to him. He breathed in the sweet air that held remnants of the apples still being harvested, maybe even a whiff of the rich Cabernet grapes that would be ready any day.

If he were to pick one time of day that captured the spirit of this valley, this would be it. The sky softly glowing off the rows of grapevines that dotted the surrounding hills, the crisp morning chill that reminded him of apple cider and fritters that were both sure to be present at today's Harvest Festival.

He remembered the events of last night, including Tessa's unease at seeing her dad pressed and groomed for his first date in decades, knowing that she had to be feeling a riot of emotions at this huge step, but seeing her tackle it well and ultimately sending him off without a tear.

She'd been melancholy initially, still stuck in her thoughts, but it hadn't taken too long for him and Elle to lull her out of that and into the spirit of the night. And later, in the kitchen just after Joe got home, there had been something that passed between him and Tessa.

He smiled as he recalled her and Elle laughing later on as they watched and rewatched the lake scene from *Dirty Dancing* half a dozen times. And even though he and Tessa didn't get another chance to be alone to talk or do whatever the spirit might have moved them to do, there had been a connection between them.

"What's that you're playing?"

Dylan startled at hearing Elle's voice behind him, unaware that she'd come out to join him on the porch. Or that he had been mindlessly strumming some chords that were representative of the mood he was in. She was in her pj's and slippers, her red hair a tangled mess that made her seem even younger than she was.

"Not really sure. It sort of came to me," he said and picked up his coffee to take a gulp as she came over and sat next to him.

"Can you show me how to play? I've always wanted to take lessons, but Mom couldn't really afford them."

Her words were familiar, as he'd grown up teaching himself back when he lived with his mom, who could barely put two cents together for a loaf of cheap bread and peanut butter in between her drug fixes, let alone guitar lessons. But he'd saved some money earned bringing the newspaper up three flights of stairs to his neighbor's house in their building, enough to buy a used guitar from the thrift store not far from them, and taught himself. This before YouTube, when anyone could pick up a few things by watching a few how-to videos.

He held the guitar out to her. "Have you ever held one before?"

She nodded. "My mom has one of Dad's old ones that I have in my room."

The only thing Dylan had to remember his old man by was his mom's drunken tirades offering a litany of the man's faults, and it kind of stung that he hadn't anything of real value of the man's. Then again, if there had been anything lying around, Dylan might have burned it in protest, his hatred and anger at Brick Jamison had been so stark back then. As Dylan had seen it, the man was the reason his whole life was crap up to that point.

Elle took his guitar in her arms, her fingers trying to find purchase on the strings while balancing the bulk of the instrument on her lap. She looked so small, so endearing and sweet that he thought what a shame it was that Brick Jamison wasn't there to see his two offspring in that moment.

"Here," he said, and helped position the guitar better, showing her where to place her fingers. After a few minutes of coaching, he was surprised at how quickly she'd picked up some of the smaller techniques he'd shown her, already playing a few chords and humming along as she did. She had a natural talent, same as what his own teacher had commented to him once he'd moved into his aunt's and started lessons.

She deserved the same.

The creaking on the porch behind him alerted him to the fact that they were being watched, and he looked over his shoulder, not surprised to see Tessa leaning against the door. With the morning sun on her face, her eyes as soft and warm as her smile, she was breathtaking, and his heart lurched in his chest with the emotions that filled him. Her hair was loose and wild around her, giving her that sweet sexiness that was beginning to drive him crazy. Instead of pj's, she was in soft blue yoga pants that hugged her curves and a slightly too small white tee shirt that rose up a little higher in the front, giving him a glimpse of that smooth skin crossing her belly. Something he wanted to run his fingers across and watch her quick intake of breath.

He grinned slowly. "Morning."

Instead of a steely-gazed response, her lips tweaked farther up into a smile that played chaos with his gut. "Morning."

He could almost sense that whatever anger and resentment and distance she'd needed to put between them had fallen away in that moment, and she was just seeing him. Not the guy who'd broken her heart. Not the rock star who'd made more mistakes than he'd like to admit.

But a guy who had done some growing up and was ready for more.

TESSA TRIED to block out the shouts of the crowd around her and focus instead on the thick layer of caramel covering the apple tied to a string in front of her. But every time she tried to take a bite, the darn thing dangled farther away.

How on earth she'd let Dylan Jamison talk her into entering the apple-eating contest she would never know. Okay, she had some inkling and she knew that she and her darn competitive spirit were as much to blame as anything.

But there had been no way she was going to let Dylan walk away with the prize when, for two consecutive years running, she'd taken the blue ribbon for her age group. She glanced over her shoulder to see that Dylan hadn't done much better and was still trying to slow the bobbing of the apple with his nose, something that elicited a giggle from her. Next to him, another contestant had gotten his teeth into the hard caramel, and immediately Tessa felt the surge of competitiveness overtake her.

She was not going to lose this. She moved forward, holding the apple between her lips before sliding her teeth in to gain purchase and ripping the flesh away.

Four and a half minutes later, her face a sticky mess of apple juice and caramel, she was announced the winner and the proud recipient of a coupon for Mack's Pancake House.

"You did it, Tessa," Elle said, coming up to hug her. "I can't believe you beat everyone else. Even the boys."

Dylan sidled next to her, holding a damp paper towel to his face. "Yeah, well, it was easy to do when half the contestants were too distracted watching you."

"Sounds like a cop-out," she said, despite the sudden heat suffusing her face at the possibility he was correct. His sly smile and that twinkle in his eye as he continued to wipe his beard only increased her temperature, but for another reason entirely.

"Mom!" Elle cried as a young woman with red hair and a wide smile came into view. "Tessa just won first place in the apple-eating contest. I didn't do so great but I got to keep mine to take home." She held up her own almost intact apple as proof.

"Sounds like I missed all the fun. Hi, I'm Lana. You must be Tessa. I hope she wasn't too much trouble."

"Not at all. We loved having her," Tessa said and handed her Elle's backpack.

"Can we do it again next weekend?" Elle asked exuberantly, looking to them both. "Maybe use that gift certificate you won for Mack's Pancake House?"

"Uh," she said, catching Dylan's eye, "I'm afraid I'm going to be back in the city by that time. How about I leave it for you and Dylan?"

"I could take you on Sunday if it's all right with your mom. Just you and me," Dylan added, trying to get Elle on board.

"I guess," she said. "But you will be back, Tessa. Right? So we can all do it again?"

"I'm sure Tessa will do her best, hon," Lana said, smiling apologetically toward Tessa. "We should probably get going. I thought I'd treat us to a movie, but it starts in half an hour. Thanks for having her, Dylan."

Elle threw herself at Tessa and gave her a hug before doing the same to Dylan. "Thanks for the best time," she said before waving and taking her mom's hand as they walked away.

"I can't believe I survived that experience," Dylan said as they watched them disappear into the crowd.

"She's a great kid. What did you expect?"

"Honestly I had no idea, but I won't deny that I was nervous going into it. The fact that we pulled it off is owed in no small part to you. I couldn't have done it myself."

"Nah. You were a pro," Tessa said as they started to walk. "Don't sell yourself short. She'd have had fun mucking horse stalls as long as she was hanging out with you. I think she might just be your number one fan."

He chuckled. "Maybe."

A couple of kids stopped in front of them, asking for a photo with him, and she stood back, watching as Dylan interacted so easily with them, asking their names and if they were local as they snapped photos with him. When they went on their way with big grins and waves, Dylan moved back to her side, not fazed in the least by the disturbance.

"Guess you get that a lot?" she asked.

"Occasionally. You get used to it."

She'd have to take his word for it. Being the center of attention was the last thing she would want.

"So, you still planning on heading back to the city on Tuesday?" Dylan asked, his hands now settled in his front pocket as they meandered through the rows of booths.

"I expect so. Of course, it all depends on whether the doctor gives my dad the okay to resume a lot of his activities —like driving, but you've seen him. He's doing pretty well. Which means I won't be needed anymore."

"It's too bad. I think he likes having you around. Not that you'll hear him admit it."

She smiled. "No, he wouldn't do that. But I've enjoyed being here, too. I forget how much I love the slower pace out here in the country."

"Maybe you can even get out here more often now that you know. Not just on the occasional holiday."

The usual guilt roiled inside. She hadn't been able to get out to the farm as much as she liked over the past few years, and now that it was about time to leave, she worried that it might be a while before she could return. "I'm going to try, but it's not as easy as it sounds. Not with my schedule."

"Sounds...stressful."

"This from the guy who goes out on the road, months at a time, and who I believe let eight months go by without seeing your aunt even once. Or at least so she told me," she added hastily in case he thought she had been stalking him or anything.

"It's true. I have been away. But as time consuming and

exhausting as it is, I love what I do. I love meeting my fans, sharing my music with them. There's nothing better than standing up there at the end of the night, feeling almost like they're all family, all out there supporting me and the band. It makes all the sacrifices worth it."

"Sounds amazing," she said, feeling a little envious at hearing this, having something he loved so much.

"It is amazing." He paused. "And because of that, I was able to convince myself it was all I needed. But I'm starting to realize that maybe I've been missing out on some other things. Connections. Real connections." He stopped, almost as if trying to put his thoughts together before continuing, his voice choked with emotion she hadn't expected. "When I heard about my dad's passing, I...I just never thought in a million years that I would care when that day came, until it did. That's when it occurred to me that I was on his same path. Not forging real relationships with anyone, always moving on, until one day I would be facing my own mortality, and other than a host of fans and an account full of money, what would I have? When Elle showed up, it got me thinking. It didn't have to be all or nothing. Maybe there could be both. That's when I realized I needed to come home. Come back to Blossom Falls and figure stuff out."

"And have you?"

"I'm getting there," he said, glancing over to her, holding her gaze for a long moment, sending her heart racing in her chest.

Dylan's phone rang from his back pocket, and he smiled in apology. "Sorry," he said, pulling it out and glancing down at the phone, his face drawing serious as he did.

It was hard for Tessa not to see the name flashing on the screen, the photo of Roxie Mann smiling out from the screen confirming his ex-girlfriend calling.

He pushed a button, declining the call, and put it back in his pocket. "I can take that later if I need to."

Tessa debated whether to let it go, pretend she hadn't seen who'd called, but her curiosity was too strong. "It was Roxie, right? Are you two talking again?" she asked as nonchalantly as possible. She didn't know why the thought that Dylan and his ex-girlfriend, the beautiful and charismatic Roxie Mann, were in contact again should annoy her since she'd made it perfectly clear her feelings toward Dylan.

"I haven't talked to her in weeks. Not since we ended things."

"Aren't you curious why she's calling you now? Do you think she's having second thoughts?"

"Nah. If I know Roxie, she's probably calling because my agent told her that I have no intention of playing with her in LA next weekend and she wants to try and talk me into it. You know, I'm starting to get hungry," he said, clearly ready to change the subject. "Want to grab a corn dog?"

Before she could answer, the sound of someone calling her name brought her attention to a familiar figure with sandy-brown hair and a tenuous smile who was heading in their direction.

"Eric?" she asked, almost not believing what she was seeing. "What are you doing here?"

"Sorry if I'm imposing on you like this. I tried you at home first but your brother—Rowan, I think it was?—told me you were here."

Feeling awkward as she stood between the two men, she struggled for what to say until Dylan stepped in, holding his hand out in greeting. "Dylan. Dylan Charles."

Since when was Dylan a name dropper?

"Eric," he said, taking Dylan's hand, not seeming to

recognize who Dylan was. He looked back to her. "I'm sorry if I interrupted you, but you left so suddenly the other night before I could gather my thoughts, and...well... I was hoping you might give me a minute of your time."

She looked over to Dylan, who was studying them both intently before clearing his throat. "I'll leave you two to talk. I can stick around for a few minutes if you need a ride back to the farm, Tessa," he added, since for today's adventure it had made sense to only take one car.

"I'm happy to give you a lift back home, Tessa," Eric offered, his tone hopeful as he stared at her.

She nodded and looked back to Dylan. "I guess I'll see you back at the house."

"All right then. Well, nice to meet you, Eric," he said and nodded before lumbering away.

They were silent for another minute as they walked, before Tessa decided to jump right in. "I'm sorry if I was abrupt the other night. I'm not very good at these kinds of things."

"No, please don't apologize. Actually, I went by your place last night to speak to you and one of your roommates told me you were here, looking after your dad. I had no idea he was in an accident."

"That's my fault. I just didn't want to burden you with my problems. But he is doing better, which is a relief. I should probably be returning to the city by Tuesday."

"I hate that you think telling me about your dad would have been burdening me. Look, I heard what you said the other night. About your career and no time for a relationship, but I want to tell you that, well, I think that we might have something that's worth waiting for."

Tessa would have to be an ice queen not to melt a little

at that. No one had ever said anything so sweet, ever just laid it out there like that. One person in particular. She met Eric's gaze, his light blue eyes studying her with such sincerity.

She shook her head as she smiled. "Why do you have to be so kind to me, after my disappearing act the other night, leaving you hanging like that? I don't really know what to say."

"Say that you'll go out with me tonight. No expectations. Let's just see if by the end of the night I can change your mind."

He'd come all the way out here. How could she say no? And maybe he was right. Maybe they could be good together. Had she not had that run-in with Dylan that first night, right on the heels of her dad's accident, would she have broken up with Eric when she had? She didn't know anymore.

She thought about Dylan and everything that she was starting to feel again. But Dylan was going to be gone again soon. Out on the road. He might be flirting with her now, enjoying a kiss while he could, but when all was said and done, he hadn't made any declaration of his feelings toward her. He could pick up tonight or tomorrow, and where would she be but broken-hearted again?

But in front of her was a guy who had all the qualities she wanted in a partner. Stability, reliability, kindness, and understanding.

She owed him at least a chance.

"All right, Eric. It's a date."

Dylan watched from the sidelines as Finn shook hands with the group of suppliers and well-wishers congratulating him on his first-place finish, his face beaming with pride as much as disbelief. From the number of orders coming in, it was clear that their anticipated expansion to the Montenegro farm's outbuildings was going to have to be pushed up if they had any hope of meeting this unexpected but appreciated demand.

In fact, they were going to be meeting with some PR firms in the next week to build up a plan as they looked to launch their product nationwide by spring. Which would mean adding a few employees to the payroll, since between his schedule and Finn's, they were going to be pretty stretched out.

He nodded to a few people who called hello and took a few pictures with those brave enough to ask him as he wandered around, all the while keeping an eye out for Tessa, who he hadn't seen since he left her earlier this afternoon with that guy. Eric.

To say Dylan was surprised by the guy's appearance was an understatement, since he'd specifically asked Tessa the other day if she had a boyfriend and she had most definitely said no. So who could he be? An ex?

Unfortunately, Tessa hadn't been around for him to ask when he arrived at the farm this evening in time to shower and get changed before he came back for tonight's event. According to Joe, Eric had come by to pick her up. Nice guy. That's what Joe had called him.

Dylan didn't know Eric personally, but he knew the type. A five-day-a-week guy, probably in the stock market, or maybe accounting. Reliable, steady. Boring as hell.

Tessa didn't need someone like that, she needed someone like...well, him.

That is, if he were in a spot where he could offer something to her or anyone, which he wasn't. Not just yet. It didn't mean that he wanted to see Tessa settle for someone in the meantime.

He was trying not to feel slighted by the fact that Tessa had gone out tonight when he had been looking forward to hanging out with her himself. But it wasn't as if she was standing him up. He hadn't exactly asked her if she'd come with him, nor would he have.

Now if they'd happened to find they needed to get here at the same time, that would have been easier for the sake of his friendship with Finn, as well as for Tessa. He wouldn't want to give her any ideas of how things were until he figured them out himself.

And until he did, he couldn't string her along, not again.

Up ahead, he saw the senior Montenegro with some familiar faces, other farmers who'd been friends with the family over the years.

"Hey, Joe," he said, coming over to say hello and see if he might have an update on Tessa's whereabouts. He'd have thought that—date or not—she would be here for this momentous occasion.

"Dylan. Good to see you," Joe said and excused himself from his friends. "I can't tell you how proud I am to see you two boys doing what you're doing. First place. Isn't that something?"

"It's all Finn, his vision and passion, that's been the driving force. I'm just along for the ride."

"Don't sell yourself short. I've seen you two working together, and it's definitely a give-and-take on both of your parts. While Finn brings his passion and agricultural knowledge, you bring your head for business and marketing. It's a good partnership."

Dylan swallowed past a lump in his throat at the man's words. "Thanks, Joe. That means a lot to me. And how are you doing tonight? Feeling all right?"

"Doing great. Nothing could have kept me from being here either way. But I will admit, I'm getting a little weary from all the walking. Sylvia McAffee saw me a few minutes ago and offered to give me a ride home. I just want to stop and tell Finn I've got a ride back, and then I'll be off."

"Sylvia?" he asked, his brow raised. "You're becoming quite the ladies' man, Joe."

"Nah. Sylvia and I go way back. We're friends is all."

"Sure. Well, don't overdo it."

"You'll let Tessa know, too, if you see her?"

After he gave Joe his assurances, the old man patted him on the back before limping over to an attractive brunette who, from the possessive way she gripped his arm, looked like she wanted to be way more than friends. Tessa was definitely not going to like that.

Dylan turned back around and stopped abruptly when he caught sight of Tessa. And it felt like all the air left his chest as he gazed at her. Instead of the wild, crazy curls and waves that had greeted him all week, tonight Tessa's raven hair was pressed into smooth, silky waves that grazed the bottom of her jawline. Her lips were a deeper berry color than her usual pink that, even from this distance, made her green eyes luminous. Gone were the casual yoga pants and the denim cutoffs, replaced with a short skirt and knee-high leather boots that were all feminine and all sexy. Just like her.

She laughed at something Eric was saying, bringing her hand up to push away a tendril of hair, and it was hard to ignore the pang of envy that ate at his gut. Eric made her laugh. That was something Dylan wanted to do. Make her laugh.

Without thought, he headed over, not quite sure what he would say but wanting her to be as aware of him as he was of her.

"Good evening," he said, watching as she turned to him, her smile less certain as she met his gaze.

"Dylan, good to see you again," Eric said politely and they shook hands again. "I have to apologize for earlier when we met. It didn't immediately click for me as to who you were, but Tessa explained everything."

Dylan smiled wryly and glanced at Tessa. "And what did Tessa explain exactly?"

"Just that you're an old friend of the family who's in town for a little downtime. I'm afraid I don't know your music all that well, but I understand it's quite popular."

He didn't know his music? What, did the guy live under a rock? Dylan studied him more closely, seeing something in his eyes as he smiled that convinced Dylan he was playing him. Eric knew very well who Dylan was, and probably had from the beginning. Not like he could call him on it.

He smiled instead. "Yeah, well, Tessa and I definitely go way back. It's been good to catch up with her these past few days and nights. But I'm afraid she never mentioned you before. You work with her at the firm or something?"

There was a flash of annoyance in the guy's eyes. And as childish as it was, Dylan took some satisfaction.

"Eric was just saying that he thought your cider was hands down the best of all he'd sampled," Tessa said, seemingly unaware of the tension between them.

"Did he?" Dylan asked. "Has Tessa had a chance to walk you through the different apple varieties that went into that brew? All of them harvested directly from the

Montenegro Farm's orchards. When you have a chance, maybe she can take you on a tour. The pond has a pretty fantastic view of the place, particularly from the old jumping rock, isn't that right, Tessa?"

Her eyes narrowed slightly. Sure, he was acting like a seventeen-year-old jealous kid, but he wanted to remind her of what had taken place on that very rock not just once but two incredible times. "Maybe later tonight I will. If Eric wants to, of course."

"I'd love to see the place."

Great. Dylan had stepped right into that one.

The last thing he really wanted was Tessa giving this guy—or any guy other than him—a tour of the property.

"So Dylan," Eric said, taking a step closer to Tessa so they were practically touching. "How long are you going to be in town? I would think that as a big-time musician, your schedule gets pretty demanding."

"It can be, sure," he said, meeting Tessa's gaze as he spoke. "But these days, I'm taking a step back from things. Want to work on my next album, spend some time with family, appreciate what I have in my life. You know how it is."

"Uh. Yeah. Sure. Well, I'll have to try and buy a couple of your songs, see what I'm missing out on." Eric turned to Tessa. "Did you mention that they're serving turkey legs at one of the booths out there? I'll admit, I've never tried one, but as hungry as I'm getting, I could probably devour an entire one myself.

"Right. We should get going," she said, almost in apology to him.

"Tessa? Before you go, could I grab you for a minute?" Dylan asked before he knew what he was about. But he couldn't let her go, couldn't see her making a mistake with this guy without saying something.

She held his gaze for a long moment, and he almost expected her to decline when she turned to Eric. "Why don't I meet you outside in a minute?"

Eric nodded and walked away, pausing to take a last look over his shoulder at Dylan before slipping outside.

"What's this about?" Tessa asked him. "And what's with all the attitude you're giving us?"

"I thought you said you didn't have a boyfriend."

"I didn't and I still don't. Eric and I have gone out on a handful of dates is all. In fact, not that it's your concern, but I told him the other night that I didn't think it was going to work out, and I ended things."

"And yet here he is."

"Yes. I guess he had a few things he wanted to say. And to see if maybe he could convince me otherwise."

"And has he? Convinced you otherwise?"

She paused. "I don't know."

He shook his head. "Man, Tessa. Don't you see? That guy is all wrong for you."

A flash of anger flickered in her eyes. "Oh, really? And how would you know who is wrong or right for me? Or maybe you could be more specific. What exactly is wrong with him?"

"Let's just say it's a gut instinct. You two have no... chemistry. No spark. You'd be bored with him in a month's time."

"You're really something, you know that? Eric is a good man. He's here tonight, fighting for me, asking me to give us one more chance. More importantly, he knows what he wants and he's not afraid to say it, which is a heck of a lot more than I could say for some people."

Touché.

But Dylan was coming into some realizations of his own these past few days. It was just taking him longer to admit the truth even when it was right in front of him.

"Okay. Then how about this. Tessa, don't go out with that guy. Go out with me. Not because he's boring and wrong for you—which is all true, by the way—but because you and I belong together. Because you and I have something that it's about damned time we explore."

Her mouth dropped open. She'd likely never imagined in a million years that he would say what he'd said. He couldn't blame her. He was still stunned himself, even though he knew it was true.

She shook her head. "That's awfully convenient for you to have this stroke of clarity right now, when Eric is waiting for me." She sighed. "Look. I don't know exactly where this is coming from but I have to go. We can talk about this later, okay?"

So her reaction was less than he expected. But she had a point. Now wasn't the time to discuss all this. "Fine. Just… just don't make any decision where that guy is concerned tonight. Okay?"

She didn't say anything, just continued to shake her head at him as she stalked away, muttering under her breath something that sounded like, "Unbelievable."

Dylan stood there another minute after Tessa disappeared outside, trying to figure out his next steps. Head back to the farm, maybe see if he could work on that new song that he'd started this morning? Sit around and wait for Tessa to come home?

Neither of those options was appealing.

Waiting around, doing nothing, letting Tessa think that he was okay with the idea of her and this guy together on a night when he'd had his own plans, something he wanted to show her.

No. He wasn't going to sit idly around. He didn't know exactly where Tessa was going to fit in his life, and he in hers, but he was getting the idea that if he didn't do something now, they'd never get the chance to find out.

TEN

TESSA WAS TRYING. SHE REALLY WAS. IT WAS THE LEAST the Eric deserved after making such an effort to be a part of her life. But she was struggling to find the excitement, the exhilaration, the...the fireworks with Eric that she felt the moment that Dylan's eyes connected with hers.

Dylan's words replayed in her mind.

Don't go out with that guy. Go out with me.

Because you and I belong together.

She'd wanted to wrap her hands around his neck and strangle him.

He had to have the worst timing in the whole entire world. Had Eric not shown up today, would he have made the same professions? How could she even take him seriously when, up to now, he hadn't so much as hinted that they could be more? Well—other than a kiss, but that was probably because he was just bored.

"How exactly do you eat this thing again?" Eric asked her as they took a seat on the end of a picnic table where they had a good view of tonight's band.

"Forget retaining any dignity and just dive right in."

He stared at it again before biting into it, taking a second to tear through the skin to the meat underneath. She laughed and offered him a napkin to catch the juice running down his chin.

"I'm glad I came," Eric said, smiling at her as he wiped it away. "It's good to see where you're from, the place and people who have influenced you."

"Me, too." She studied Eric, noting again all the features he possessed that checked off all the right boxes. He wasn't going to be spooked when things got too serious. He wasn't going to run.

And with time, maybe she could see herself falling in love with him. He'd be easy to fall into a rhythm with if she wanted to.

The question was, did she want to?

The band finished their song and they excused themselves for a quick break before exiting the stage.

"You have to help me eat this thing. It's the least you can do so I can salvage some of my dignity."

Yeah, he was pretty sweet. Maybe not a suave as Dylan, but he was kind and considerate.

But she'd be lying if she said there was any magic between them.

The sound of excitement ran through the crowd as the band reappeared on the stage, only this time with another person in tow, a guitar already strapped around his neck.

Dylan took a step forward, grabbing the microphone. "Good evening, Blossom Falls."

The crowd went crazy when it became clear Dylan's intentions were to play a song for them.

"Thank you. The band here's been gracious enough to

let me join them up here tonight for a song. It's one of the first songs of mine that ever played on the radio, so it's something that's near and dear to my heart. You probably have heard it a time or two. I wrote it with one person in mind, and I thought it was only fitting that, being here with you all, I play it again tonight."

He strummed at the strings, the opening immediately recognizable to Tessa, who for years had wondered if he'd thought of her as he wrote it. It had gutted her every time it came on, and she steeled herself against the pain that hearing it again would cause. But it was different somehow, especially as he drawled out the opening line, and his eyes locked on hers, as if he'd known where she was sitting all along.

She swallowed, trying to still the rapid beating of her heart, the ache that his sultry voice brought on.

It wasn't our time.

It wasn't meant to be.

But maybe,

Just maybe,

Someday she'll come back to me.

He wasn't playing fair. He couldn't just come back to town and play that song, here, now. And he couldn't play it and turn those brown eyes to her in that special way that had her heart hammering so loudly in her chest.

And like that, the last pieces of the wall she'd built around her heart seemed to be falling away, and tears filled her eyes.

"Tessa? You okay?" Eric asked.

She looked at him, knowing that no matter how much time they had together, she would never feel the same sweeping array of emotions that Dylan evoked in her. And to pretend that was okay with her, that it was enough, wasn't fair to her and certainly wasn't fair to him.

"I will be. But first, I think we need to talk."

TESSA SHUT THE CAR DOOR, waving a permanent good-bye to Eric, who attempted to smile back before driving away. It hadn't been easy to tell him what she did, but it was the right thing to do.

She turned around, ready to head into the house when she noticed the figure sitting on the top porch step. Dylan.

"Hey," he said.

She didn't reply, instead coming to take a seat next to him.

"Surprised to see you home so early," he said. "Something wrong?"

"Really? That's how you want to play this, even after that stunt you pulled? Do you want to tell me what you were trying to say in playing that song tonight?"

Tessa needed to hear him say it. She could have misinterpreted his meaning entirely. Maybe he had just wanted to please the crowd. Maybe just wanted to set Eric in his place for not knowing who he was. It might not have had anything to do with her.

"I would have told you had you stuck around after the song, but you left."

She'd left because she needed to speak with Eric in private. She'd owed him at least that. "Well, I'm here now. What were you going to tell me?"

"I think it's something that would be best if I just showed you." He stood up, reaching his hand out to her. She hesitated for only a second before letting him help her up, his hand feeling good as it held hers for that quick moment, before she took hers back, not yet sure where things were going.

They were in the truck a minute later, heading in the direction of the main highway when he suddenly took a left at the fork. The only thing at the end of this road was... "Are you taking me out to see the Wallace place?"

Dylan just smiled, not offering any hints.

She settled back in the seat, trying to be patient even as her nerves were getting more and more strained under the pressure of everything that remained unsaid between them.

They pulled up to the house, but where she expected darkness, she was surprised to see a light on over the porch. "Is someone here? I thought Dad said something about the new owner living in Pasadena?"

"I actually have it on pretty good authority that the owner lives right here in town."

The way he was grinning that dopey grin made her look at him more closely. He didn't mean... "You didn't buy the Wallace place, did you?" she asked, getting out of the truck.

"Guilty as charged."

She stared back to the farmhouse, actually at a loss for words. "I— Wait. You bought his place? Whatever would possess you to do that?"

He came around the truck to stand next to her, staring out at the house, and she stepped forward, too, coming to stand next to him. "I've been thinking about finding a place of my own for some time. Remember how Finn and I were talking about maybe buying the apple orchards for the business? Well, Jasper found the current owner, but they're only interested in selling it all or nothing. And the answer became obvious. This place? This town? It all made sense."

"There have to be hundreds of other places you could have chosen, grander houses than this old place."

"All true. But from the moment I saw the place again the other day, standing about where we are now, I knew it was meant to be mine."

Dylan had bought the Wallace place.

Her incredulity wasn't based on her thinking it was a bad choice. Quite the opposite. Tessa had always loved this place. Not as large as the Montenegros' farmhouse, it still had character and plenty of space inside for her and the three dogs and two cats she envisioned for herself at ten years old. As kids, they all used to play hide and seek inside, there being no short supply of small closets and doorways linking all the rooms together.

And now Dylan was the owner.

"So? What do you think?"

A wave of anger and resentment hit her and she struggled to keep from screaming. "I think—I think that you're really something."

He studied her. "I don't understand. You're...mad at me?"

"You're darn right I'm mad. For all those years you were so adamant that this place wasn't for you, that this life here wasn't for you." That she, Tessa, wasn't for him, she thought but fortunately had the sanity not to say out loud. "And when you left Blossom Falls, I learned to accept the fact that you and I were just...different. That it had been in your nature to want more, a different life, a less settled life. But now you're standing here and telling me you not only want to plant roots, but you want to do it here? In a house so close that I could see it from my bedroom window if I was of a mind to look."

Instead of firing off an angry retort, however, Dylan was

just standing there smiling at her, giving her a good urge to kick him in the shin.

"Let me understand this," he drawled. "You're angry not because I bought the house and plan to settle down but because I'm doing all of this now."

"No," she snapped, but realized denial was futile. She sighed. "Maybe. I don't know."

He stepped in front of her view of the house so she had to look at him and those eyes that were filled with a warm light and something else. Hope?

"Growing up like I did with my mom, the only thing that made sense to me was my music. It was the one thing where my efforts actually were rewarded. Where the more time I spent practicing, the more I could see life and beauty taking shape by my own hard work."

Tessa didn't know the extent of what life had been like for Dylan with his mom, but she knew that it had gotten pretty bad leading up to her death. When he'd shown up at his aunt's an angry and hurt twelve-year-old boy, not wanting to care about anyone or let them care about him, Tessa had realized he needed someone to look after him, and that person was going to be her. With time and nurturing from those around him, Dylan had changed. Learned to accept praise and love and laughter. Her love for him changed, too, getting bigger and brighter and all too consuming even though she hadn't always understood what she was feeling.

"Even as a kid, I'd vowed that I would do anything, take every avenue I had to to make my music my future," he continued, taking her hand and slipping it into his own. "When I got to Blossom Falls, I found a sense of belonging and love that I'd never had, and that I embraced even though I never let go of my dream of being a musician.

What I didn't expect, however, was...you. You always looked at me, even at nine years old, as something better and brighter than I saw myself. Watching you grow up, I felt almost what I thought was a brotherly affection. Until that Christmas I saw you in a way that, if Finn or the rest of your family knew, would leave me pulverized. I knew I was in trouble and that the best course of action was to stay away before I did something stupid."

Tessa remembered the Christmas he was talking about. She'd been sixteen and had been waiting to see Dylan ever since his aunt told them he would be coming home from his first year of college for the winter break. She thought she'd felt something in the way he looked at her, the way he couldn't stop looking at her, and she'd felt deliriously happy and terrified at the same time. But then something came up and he'd taken off the day after Christmas. It was strangely exhilarating to know that he hadn't been as immune as she thought he must have been.

"Those two weeks when I came back after you lost your mom, I knew I was walking a dangerous line between my feelings and the boundaries that had to stay firmly in place between us. You were so sad, so lost, and all I knew was that I couldn't leave you. So I stayed and we spent more time together, really talked together, and despite myself and my big dreams, I fell hard for you enough that I finally took leave of my senses and kissed you that night. And that kiss..." He shook his head. "It was the best thing that had ever happened to me. It made me feel things that I hadn't realized were possible. And it scared the hell out of me, so I did the only thing I thought made sense at the time. I left. But I never stopped thinking about you. And these past few days, being with you again? It's the only thing that's made sense to me in a long time."

Tessa felt stupid tears cloud her eyes. Knowing he was speaking his truth. Knowing that it was as true for her, too. She had thought she hated him over all these years. But the love? It had always been there. And for the first time, she believed that maybe it wasn't as one-sided as she'd feared.

"Look, Tessa. I don't know what the future is going to be. Where you or I will be. I just know that right now, being with you feels right. I spent ten years wondering what would have happened if I'd made a different choice that night, and now that I'm back here again, I don't want to risk another ten years going by, or wondering what would have happened if I'd been brave enough to tell you what I was feeling. That there's something between us, something I think could be really good. And if you're up to it, I'd like to give it a real go."

Tessa took a step back, needing the space from him and the warmth and promise in his eyes to put her thoughts together. "It would be easy, so easy, to say yes. But it isn't that simple anymore. We have different lives now. You're a musician. You're going to be out on the road eventually. And I have a life, friends, a home, and a job in the city. I just don't see how that would work."

"It's worth trying, don't you think? And San Francisco isn't the end of the world. I'll visit you when I can, and you can come and see me, too. Whether here at the farm or out on the road. You know, those tour busses are far more comfortable than you might expect." He took a step forward again and closed the space, only this time the truck was against her back and she was left with nowhere to retreat. "I don't want to walk away wondering what if anymore. Why shouldn't we give it a shot and see what comes of it?"

She'd run out of excuses and they both knew it. Now it

was a matter of answering what was in her heart, something she'd been good at ignoring these past few years.

Tessa reached her hand up, touching his face. But words wouldn't come, and instead she used the only thing she could to tell him her answer. She kissed him. The only true expression of emotion they'd ever shared the precious two times before.

She heard his intake of breath as her lips covered his, the shock as he froze for the barest moment, before he accepted everything she was telling him without speaking a word, and his hands cupped her face as he brought her in closer. Unlike the previous kisses, the first coming from wonder and curiosity as they tested their feelings for each other, the second from unsaid emotions that nearly overwhelmed them, this kiss was the most real of all. Accepting their past, the pain that their separation caused them for years, and an understanding that no matter how hard they'd tried to pretend they didn't care, the person in their arms was the one person they could never escape from.

And who, maybe, they no longer needed to.

"You're not holding out on me, are you, Lynn?" Tessa teased the older woman selling kiwi fruits Sunday morning at the farmers' market.

Despite having gotten maybe four hours of sleep last night from the time she and Dylan finally parted in the hall to the moment she'd opened her eyes this morning and the memories of everything that had taken place the night before flooded over her, Tessa was feeling more awake than she'd felt in a long time.

"Would I give my favorite customer anything but the best?" Lynn said.

Dylan always liked desserts, fruit tarts being high on the list if she remembered correctly. "Give me the full bag then."

Was she really standing here thinking about ways to Dylan Jamison's stomach—and heart? She glanced over to see Dylan talking on his phone with Elle, his blond hair shining more golden under the morning sunlight. Combined with the aviator glasses he wore to shield his eyes from the glare, he looked very Hollywood. Something that hadn't escaped her notice—or the notice of the women around them, who weren't bothering to try and hide their stares.

She sighed softly, still unable to believe the culmination of events that had taken place in the space of a day. She, Tessa Montenegro, a woman who didn't take chances—particularly with her heart—had decided to take that leap of faith and accept Dylan's offer to see where this thing between them could go. Every minute in his company had felt almost dreamlike, and she'd wanted to pinch herself to see if it were real.

Except when he was kissing her. Those moments—the many, many moments they'd had since he first told her how he felt—were the ones that felt most real. How couldn't they when they served as a reminder of why no one had ever compared to Dylan Jamison before or after that first fateful kiss?

"Here you go, honey," Lynn said, bringing her from her reverie as she handed Tessa the bag of fruit. "I hear that you've been helping Jasper with Claudia Nunn's case against the gas company."

"Oh, that's overstating my involvement a bit. I'm afraid

there wasn't really much I could do that Jasper hadn't already done."

"Well, I've been meaning to come into Jasper's for some time to talk about getting my estate in order, but since he was married to my sister all those years ago, I've been a little on the fence. Now, if you were going to be there more frequently helping him out, I might stop in and get things moving."

"That's so sweet of you to think of me," Tessa said, touched that Lynn thought of her in such high regard. "But I'm only going to be in town for a couple more days. I was only here to help my dad out, and since he's on the mend, I'll probably be leaving day after tomorrow." At least as long as the doctor gave him the okay to resume more of his every day tasks at his visit tomorrow. "Now knowing Jasper as I do, history not withstanding, I know he'll do his best for you. You should call him."

A warm hand wrapped around her waist, and her gut sucked in as she shivered from his touch.

"Here. Let me," Dylan said and took the bag filled with fruit from her.

Lynn smiled conspiratorially at Tessa. "Now you take care of yourself, Tessa. Don't be a stranger."

"I won't. Thanks, Lynn."

Dylan's hand moved from her waist and took her hand in his as they walked, and he placed the bulk of the day's purchases in the other hand. Neither of them said anything, instead just enjoying each other's presence as they strolled through the stalls of produce and farm-made goods.

Being here around people she'd known since she was a baby, catching up on news and gossip felt oddly comforting. Familiar. Gratifying. What once had felt stifling as she had grown up with everyone knowing hers and the rest of the

Montenegro clan's business now felt like a big hug from a town that really, genuinely cared about her—about everyone.

"Why was Elle calling?" she asked, curious as to the reason for the early morning call.

"Appears she already wants to confirm our weekend plans for pancakes. She also wants me to help her work on a song for an upcoming talent show at the school."

"That's so sweet. You told her yes, right?"

"Told her can't imagine a better way to spend our time together. She wants you to put the date on your calendar, too, by the way. It's the Monday before Thanksgiving."

"Monday?" Tessa couldn't imagine a worse day to try and get away from work, what with Thanksgiving just a few days away. "I will make it happen," she said with determination, ignoring the twinge of anxiety she had just thinking about the excuses she'd need to make at work to sneak away. But this was Elle and it was important.

"There's something else I was thinking about. Now that I'm going to be the proud owner of not just a house but also an apple orchard and a rather large, unused barn, I have some decisions to make, contractors to meet with..."

The possibilities swirled in her mind. "I hope you're going to go with white on the clapboards. Maybe black...or even green accents. And you definitely will have to open that kitchen, maybe look at getting an island."

He laughed. "I see you have a few opinions already, all of which I want to hear about. But first I was thinking about the barn. I'm not really much of a guy who sees himself getting up at the crack of dawn to feed the chickens or pigs or whatever it is farmers keep. There were a few other possibilities I was considering and I wanted your opinion."

"Okay, shoot."

"First, depending on how successful Rocking Blues Cider becomes, it could be an interesting place to turn into a tasting room. Maybe set up a little shop where we sell the cider as well as some local products to tourists."

"Is that what you'd want, though? I would think buying a place out here in the country was an escape for you from all of that attention," she said, even as the possibilities flowed. The old barn, faded red but still representative of the farm's origins, would be amazing as a tasting room. The rafters could be painted and the whole ceiling opened up with lights strung up during the holidays—"

"There's enough land between the barn and the house right now that, with a good fence and a reworking of the road around the place, it could still keep the house secluded and private. Which brings me to the other prospect. Seeing as how the town is in such dire need of a place for all the future artists to be nurtured and taught, what if we turn it into the community's next art studio? Only, maybe we could expand it into a performing art studio. One where kids like you could learn to paint and express their creativity through painting and drawing, while kids like Elle, who don't have the means to afford otherwise, could take free music lessons. And if there's an interest, maybe there'll be some room for a dance studio or maybe a theater club."

Tessa thought she was going to burst at the possibilities that Dylan was painting for her. Of young artists being inspired to be the next Edward Hopper or Georgia O'Keefe as they basked under the tutelage of people in the community who saw the value in what they could do. Of young musicians and dancers having someone to believe in them and show them how they could make their dreams a reality. It was too late for her, perhaps, but others could be inspired.

"I think—" Her tears welled up again, and she laughed because she'd turned into such a baby in the space of twelve hours. "I think that last bit? About the community center sounds perfect."

Her excitement was so sudden that—without thinking of who saw her—she threw herself into his arms and planted a long kiss on his lips. She laughed as he whipped her around before finally setting her down and—even as dozens of people were watching—this time settling a more leisurely kiss on her that, had he not been holding her up, might have sent her to the ground in a puddle, barely aware of the dozens of flashes going off just over her shoulder.

All she cared about was the sun on her face, the tingling warmth of her lips from his kiss, and the man smiling down on her like she was the only thing important in the world.

He set her down, taking a moment to clear a tendril of hair from her eyes.

"So much for your keeping a low profile," she said, her heart light and free of any doubt. Life was definitely looking up.

Dylan's phone rang and he slipped his hand from hers to get it. "Sorry. Aunt Daphne's supposed to get back with me about dinner tonight," he said apologetically.

But the number on the screen wasn't Daphne.

"You probably should just get it," Tessa told him. "Otherwise she'll probably keep calling."

"If you're sure you don't mind."

She shook her head and smiled even though she didn't feel as casual about it as she pretended. But his avoiding his ex wasn't going to make her go away. Best to see what she wanted so they could move on.

Leaning down, he kissed her quickly on the lips before answering, "Hey, Roxie."

Needing a distraction, Tessa headed over to the Barnsworth family's stand, where she checked out the array of pickled vegetables and canned marmalades, even as bits and pieces of Dylan's conversation reached her.

Relax, Tessa.

He didn't choose Roxie. He chose you.

She just had to have some faith.

ELEVEN

Dylan's hope was high after experiencing the best twenty-four hours of his life as he answered Roxie's call. Tessa had been right. The woman was rabid when she wanted to be and was unlikely to stop calling until she said whatever it was she had to say. He could be patient with her.

"Good morning, handsome. How's country life treating you? You just about bored to death and ready to join the living?" Roxie asked, her tone flirty and playful, very different from the last time they'd talked, when accusations and bitter resentment were all that was between them.

He rubbed his forehead. "Hey, Roxie. Life's treating me pretty good. How are things going with you?"

"It could be better. You could stop toying with me about playing at my concert next Saturday and just accept what we both know you want to do. What your agent is dying for you to do."

"Wish I could, but I'm pretty busy out here. Have a lot on my plate. Besides, you know as well as I do that you don't need me performing with you for that concert to be great."

"Of course it will be great. With you it will be unforgettable. When we're up there on that stage together, just like that night in Seattle, it's magic." She sighed. "But that's not the only reason I'm calling."

That he figured. Her agent could have made the call if it was just his participation at the concert that Roxie wanted. He waited.

"The truth is...I miss you. I miss us."

He didn't say anything at first, trying to decide how to respond without sounding like a jerk. Because the truth was that, despite nearly two years together, he had found it remarkably easy to go on without her in his life. If he was honest with himself, it had always felt like they were just killing time with each other, not really moving toward anything real. That wasn't to say he hadn't enjoyed her company, and she had been a good friend. So it wasn't too much of a stretch for him to offer her some gesture. "I miss you, too, Rox. We had some good times together."

"I'm so happy to hear you say that, baby. I think we could still make this work."

"What happened to Kevin?" he asked, referring to the bass player she'd been canoodling with the past few months —both before and after their breakup.

"Kevin and I are over. You know the only reason I started seeing him was because I felt you were taking me for granted. I wanted to make you see me again."

"Well, I definitely saw you. You know you could have just told me that without using Kevin."

"I know and I'm trying to work on that. If you could come back to LA, I would have a better chance of showing you just how sorry I am. What do you say? Can you forgive me, give us one more chance?"

"Forgiveness isn't even a question. I was as much to

blame as you for how things went down. But, Rox...I'm sorry. Nothing has changed since we last talked. You and me? We were never a good fit."

There was silence on the other end, and he was certain his response was the last one she'd expected. He glanced over to find Tessa studying him, undoubtedly hearing bits and pieces of the conversation. She was what was important right now, and now that he had reaffirmed for Roxie what they both already knew, it was time to move on.

"Hey, Roxie. I've got to go. You take care of yourself, okay?" He waited for her reply but was met instead with the call being disconnected.

He headed over to Tessa, offering her a reassuring smile. "Looks like you've added a few more things to our bounty," he said, referring to the Mason jars in her arms. "What do we have here?"

"Marmalade. I thought that Quinn and Anna might appreciate some when I get back home." Her eyes were uncertain as she studied him. "Everything okay?"

"Everything is great. Nothing for you to worry about." He held one of the bags open. "Go ahead. Put it in. I'll carry it."

She carefully placed them in the bags, not immediately saying anything.

"You want to know what Roxie called about?"

She met his gaze again. "No. If you say it's over with her, then I'm okay with things."

"Of that you should have no doubt." He held his arms open, beckoning her to step into his embrace. She smiled a little shyly up at him but did so. "The only woman I want in my arms, Tessa Montenegro, is you."

He felt the tension that she denied having melt away. See?

They could do this. They could get through the detours that would likely arise, as long as they communicated and trusted in each other.

———

TESSA HOPPED out of the truck a couple hours later and ran over to the driver side to say good-bye.

"You sure you don't want to come over and say hello? I'm sure Aunt Daphne would love to have you," Dylan said, leaning out through the open window.

"I should probably stick around here. Get dinner for my dad. But you go and enjoy yourself. Tell her I said hi."

"I will. I guess I'll see you later tonight," he said and kissed her.

"That's pretty risky of you, sir," she teased. "If Finn or Dad or any one of my other brothers saw that, you would have a lot of explaining to do."

"You're worth the risk," he said and winked.

With a wave, she saw him off, standing in the driveway a few more minutes.

Silly. But she already was missing him.

For kicks, she pulled her phone out, ready to text him something overly sappy.

Having placed the phone on its quiet mode when they went to the restaurant for lunch earlier, she was surprised to see the page of alerts and notifications flashing.

What on earth?

Curious, she scrolled through them. Her Instagram account that usually never saw any action was flooded with the most alerts. Her texts had also blown up, and she saw she'd missed some calls from her roommates. No missed calls from her dad or brother, so that was a relief.

Guess she would start with the voicemail that it looked like Anna had left first.

You are in big trouble. You and Dylan Charles? When the heck did that happen? And why are Quinn and I the last people on earth to hear about this? You had better call us STAT so we can get all the dirty details. And I mean all the details.

Tessa laughed at the implication in Anna's tone.

How on earth had they heard the news? Well, since it was her Instagram account that was still actively notifying her of updates and messages, she might as well start there. She opened it up and scrolled through, trying to make sense of all the messages and mentions she was seeing. Particularly why people she didn't even know were calling her such horrible, mean things. It took her a few more seconds to reach the original post that, the moment she saw it, she knew was the cause.

Someone had caught her and Dylan earlier today in the square kissing. It wasn't actually a bad picture. Seeing it made her remember all the feelings of love and happiness she'd had in that moment.

What had started to stir up trouble, however, was when Roxie Mann reposted the same picture to her account barely an hour before with a singular caption.

I guess space apart was code for moving on. Thanks for nothing. Xoxo, Roxie

She'd already had over forty thousand likes to her post.

Another text flashed across her screen, this one from Quinn.

Whatever you do, do NOT open your Instagram account. It isn't worth it. Call us when you can. Love you.

Too late.

The joy she'd been experiencing just a minute before

was gone, and she fought against the sickening feeling growing in her stomach. As if sensing her emotional upheaval, her phone rang. It was Anna again.

Without hesitating, she brought the phone to her ear. "Hey."

"Hey yourself. Quinn and I have been going crazy for the past hour trying to reach you. You and Dylan? How could you hold out on us like that?"

Tessa paused. "It's kind of a long story. Can it wait until I get back home?"

"What's going on, Tessa? Are you okay? Don't tell me you went on to Instagram." She heard some shuffling, and a moment later, Quinn got on the phone. "Oh, Tessa. I told you not to read that. It's just sick rabid fans who don't have any life of their own. It will pass. Give it some time. Will you still be coming home on Tuesday? We miss you out here."

"I expect so. Dad's definitely doing better," she said. With all the developments with Dylan in the past day, the thought of leaving here and returning home didn't fill her with the same relief as it usually did.

"That's good news, right?" Anna asked, probably sensing her feelings.

"Yeah. Of course," she said, trying to sound happier than she felt at the prospect.

They chatted for a few more minutes as Anna and Quinn took turns telling her stories about their own hectic lives in the past few days while Tessa had been gone, successfully helping her find something to laugh about.

When it came time to say good-bye, she listened as they each warned her not to go on Instagram and to remove the app entirely from her phone until things died down, something she assured them she'd do straightaway.

Hanging up, though, the temptation was there to see if the hate-mongering continued. She opened it again.

Yep. All still the same.

Fat cow.

Nobody.

Slut.

There was more, but this time sanity took hold, and she closed it and pressed down on the app until she deleted it.

With a little relief but a heavy heart, she climbed the porch steps and slipped quietly into the sanctuary of the house.

———

DYLAN SHIFTED the weight of the box of things his aunt had sent home with him until he could reach the door at the farm and push it open. He had no idea of the box's contents, not really feeling up for the task while his aunt was looking on, particularly when a call from Finn came in telling him about Roxie's Instagram post and demanding he get back to the farm immediately.

It looked like the cat was out of the bag as to his and Tessa's relationship, and it was time for him to have the conversation with his best friend that he should have had ten years before. But first, he needed to see Tessa and make sure she was doing okay in light of this turn of events.

Despite it only being eight on a Sunday night, the kitchen was still and quiet, the dinner dishes put away and a solitary light on above the stove. Dylan set the box down and went in search of Tessa. She was sitting on the couch with her dad in the family room, a tub of rocky road ice cream between them and *Dirty Dancing* playing on the television.

Tessa looked up when she saw him, a tentative smile crossing her face. "Hey, stranger."

"Hey yourself. I hear that you've had a rough time. Why didn't you call me? I could have been here for you."

"It's okay. A gallon of ice cream, a viewing of my favorite movie, and time with my dad were the perfect medicine."

"And she means in that order," Joe said. He started to get up, grunting as he made the effort. "I'll leave you two alone. I'm sure you have some things to discuss.

"Actually, I wanted to talk to you. Can you hang on a quick minute?"

The older man raised a brow and settled back in, nodding to him to go on.

"I wanted to assure you that my intentions where Tessa are concerned are honorable and not taken lightly. She means everything to me and has for some time. I only wish I'd been honest with her, with you, with the whole family before now."

Joe stared at him a long moment and Dylan swallowed hard. He didn't look happy. But just as suddenly, the man's face broke into a smile and he chuckled. "Son, I've known how you feel about Tessa since you first sat out on my porch and shared your root beer popsicle with her when she was nine years old. I've been waiting for you to recognize the truth. If it means anything, Tessa's mom thought as much, too."

Tessa sat up and stared at her dad. "Mom knew?"

"Sure did. We'd have had to be blind not to see you two had a connection the moment you met. It was much like the connection your mom and I had from the start."

Dylan's shoulders lost some of their tension at the elder

Montenegro's acceptance, even while he knew he still had the siblings to reckon with.

Tessa leaned her head against her dad, smiling. She would be in good hands for a few more minutes. At least until he got the conversation with Finn out of the way.

He cleared his throat. "And Finn? Have you seen him?"

The older man smiled. "Sure. He's waiting for you in the barn. They all are."

Of course they were.

"I'll be back soon. I hope."

Sure enough, Dylan caught sight of three of the five Montenegro brothers as soon as the barn door creaked open. Even without Aidan and Liam, they were a terrifying force to face. They remained silent as he walked in, their faces unreadable.

"I'm guessing you all probably have questions about my intentions regarding your sister."

"Damn right," Rowan said, his arms crossed in front of his body. His green eyes spit with anger and fire, very much like Tessa's.

"Why don't you start by telling us what your intentions are," Declan said from his seat in front of one of the vats of cider, a little calmer than his younger brother as he picked up a glass of cider and took a drink. He gestured to another chair next to Finn.

Dylan cast a wary glance to Finn, who sat in silence, his expression reserved.

"I don't ordinarily sit down with a woman's brothers and lay out what I'm hoping for from the relationship,"

Dylan said as he slid onto the metal folding chair, trying to bring some humor to the situation.

But no one grinned.

Immediately, he changed his tone as he leveled with the guys who were more like brothers to him than anything else. "Look. I know that for you guys, this relationship seems to have sprung up from nowhere. You have no idea if this is just a fling or if it's something more."

"You have had a habit of making headlines with a crop of different women over the years," Declan said. "Can you blame us for questioning your motives when you're not exactly known for long-lasting relationships? And this is Tessa we're talking about."

"I can't deny that I've had a lot of attention on my love life over the years. Some true, some not. But none of those women could ever hold a candle to Tessa. The truth is, I think I've been falling for her since the moment I first met her. Only, growing up together, I was clueless as to what those feelings meant. It took me a while to realize what Tessa meant to me. She's..." He shook his head, trying to find the words to describe her. "She's special. She makes me believe in things I didn't know were possible. I love her and I promise you all now that I'll do everything in my power to protect her. Make her feel safe and loved. Permanently."

No one said anything at first, all mulling over his words. Finn spoke first. "How do we know you're not going to get cold feet and run out on her again, like you did before?"

Now it was his turn to be surprised. How the hell had Finn known?

Rowan and Declan seemed just as surprised from the looks on their faces, but they held their tongues when they saw the intensity on Finn's face as he studied Dylan.

No matter how or when Finn had found out, the question was valid. "I was stupid and immature, didn't fully appreciate what I had. And truthfully, I thought Tessa would be better off without me. She had a future before her, and I didn't want to go messing with that. Other than that, all I can ask is that if Tessa is willing to give me a chance, you all will, too."

Finn rubbed his jaw. "Guess time will tell. But let me be clear. If you hurt her, I will break both your legs, partnership not withstanding. She deserves only the best man, and I guess...well, I guess I can't think of anyone better than you."

Dylan smiled and took the hand his friend offered. He realized the room was still silent and he turned to Rowan and Declan. The brothers glanced at each other another long moment, and Dylan waited, holding his breath. Whatever silent conversation the brothers had seemed to be over as they finally returned his gaze. And grinned.

"Tessa's got a pretty good head on her shoulders," Declan said. "If she thinks you're worth taking a chance on, then we don't see any reason to object."

Rowan came forward with a full pint of cider and handed it to him. "But Finn's right. We will break your legs if you do anything to hurt her."

Dylan fought back a grin as he held up his glass to them. "Fair enough."

DYLAN STEPPED BACK into the family room half an hour later, no worse for wear after his meeting with the Montenegro brothers. Tessa was still resting on the couch, but the ice cream and her dad were both absent.

"You seem to be in one piece. Are there any internal

injuries I should be aware of?" she asked when she caught sight of him.

He joined her, resting his arm around her and bringing her in closer to his side. He thought about all the times they'd sat together on this couch over the years, but never so intimately. It felt nice. It felt right. And now he didn't have to hide his true feelings for Tessa anymore. Not just from his friends or Tessa, but himself.

"You going to tell me what happened out there, or do I need to call Finn in to explain himself?" Tessa asked.

"They gave us a toast," he said. "Toasted our future."

She sat up, tucking her knees under her as she turned to stare at him. "A...toast? That's all?"

He nodded. "Apparently after they made me sweat it for a while, they all claimed to have seen it coming a long time ago. Not to say there wasn't a moment when they gave me a warning to make sure I didn't hurt you, but most of the time, we just...drank."

She burst out into laughter. "You should have seen your face when you walked out of here earlier. Dad and I had a bet you'd probably pass out before you reached the barn."

"Glad to hear my terror caused you all such glee," he said, but he smiled and took her hand, rubbing his thumb across the skin. "Now to other events not so humorous. Tessa, I am sorry that Roxie made that post and that her fans are coming after you. It's unfair and childish and I...I don't have any other excuses for her. I'd call her on it but that's probably exactly what she wants, me to call and open that door again. But I've talked to my agent and he'll be reaching out to hers."

She leaned back to rest her head on the couch and gazed at him, trying to put on a brave smile for him, but he could see in her eyes the pain it was causing. It nearly broke him.

"Come here," he said, pulling her again into his arms. "This will blow over, I promise. And if not, we'll just have to change the narrative. You and I are meant to be together, and with time, everyone will see that."

"That's not very reassuring," she said, laughing nervously against his shoulder. "I'm not used to having my relationships up for scrutiny. I don't even share stuff like that with my family, let alone the thousands of people who've already sounded off."

"It can be challenging, I'll admit. People thinking they know better than you about your own life, not to mention the trolls who only want to stir up trouble. But there are also some good people out there. People who love my music and care about my life, and they'll only want the best for us both. You'll see."

"It will be an adjustment, but I guess you're worth the trouble."

"Oh? I'm worth it?" He squeezed her waist, immediately earning a squeal of laughter as she tried to get away. "You can do better than that."

"Guess time will tell," she said instead.

He made a lunge for her again, loving the sound of her laughter filling the room. When she'd finally cuddled back on his lap, breathless and flushed, he took joy in lacing her hand in his, her head leaning against his chest.

"This? This is what I'm going to miss the most when you leave. You're sure we can't talk you into staying one more week?"

"Afraid not. Not if I want to keep my job."

"Would it be too needy of me if I stop by and take you to dinner Tuesday night? I'm meeting with a couple different architects to discuss the designs for the house and barn. We can make it for however late as you need, since I know you're going to need to put in some long hours of catch-up. I'll take a midnight supper as long as it's with you."

"I think I can make it work. But I should warn you. My roommates are going to lose their minds when they see you. We'll be lucky to get away at all."

He leaned down and kissed the top of her head. "I look forward to it. Even it we end up just ordering takeout."

She seemed to consider it, a smile playing around her mouth. "Then again, if I don't tell them you're coming, there's a better chance I'll have you all to myself."

He moved a strand of hair from her eyes. "I can hardly argue with that."

TWELVE

Tessa finished the spoonful of salted caramel ice cream Tuesday evening and dropped it into the pint before pushing it away in case she felt compelled to eat another bite. If she drowned her stress in ice cream like this for much longer, she would have to be rolled out of here.

Her phone buzzed and she stared warily at it, wondering what bad news could be on its way now. But it was only a text message from Dylan, and she grabbed it with relief.

Finished early. Should I keep myself busy another couple hours or are you ready for my charming company?

She quickly typed her response.

Now.

She didn't dare try to say more or let him know the turmoil she was in. How, despite everything she'd worked for these past few years, it might all be done thanks to a silly photo. Apparently the partners of the firm didn't like to see their grieving employees who were supposed to be playing nursemaid to an ill parent out fraternizing with rock stars.

Pending an investigation, she was suspended for the next three days.

Reeling from the news, she'd barely managed to keep her dignity as she strode down the hall and elevator until she reached the fresh air, where she was hit with a barrage of photographers. Somehow they'd figured out not only where she was employed but—as she saw when she arrived home—her house address.

It had been oddly unsetting to have the cameras trained on her, hoping for something they could print and subject her to more scrutiny. Which was why, after she'd arrived back in the safety of the three-bedroom duplex, she'd locked the door and planted herself on the couch wondering how things had gotten so crazy.

By the time Dylan knocked on the door twenty minutes later, she was a ball of nerves from wondering if she was making a mistake in letting him come here when her partners had suspended her for fraternizing with him in the first place. Cautiously, she peered out, confirming it was him and the blessed lack of photographers before grabbing him and pulling him inside.

Dylan looked bemused, rubbing his arm from where she'd tugged on him. "That wasn't exactly the kind of greeting I was hoping for. Are we under attack out there?"

"You could say that."

He studied her face, his own growing serious as he realized her distress. "Hey. What's going on? You're staying off social media, right?"

"I am, but even that is killing me since I'm torn between wanting to know what's being said and remaining blissfully ignorant of the same." She nodded outside. "Then there were photographers waiting outside the office and when I got home today. Which was almost as bad as the moment I was called into the partners' meeting, where I was informed I was suspended."

"They suspended you?" he asked, sounding both confused and angry on her behalf. "Wait. Step back," he said and led her to the couch. "What did they say?"

She relayed to him what the partners had said first thing when she arrived to work, how they questioned her integrity when she initially said she had to take emergency leave, and how in light of recent photos, they wanted to get more information before they made their decision.

"Idiots. Treating you like that. Damn it." Dylan sat forward, staring in front of him. "This is all my fault. I should have known that Roxie was a loose cannon and been more careful. Made her think the entire breakup was her decision."

"Hey. This isn't on you," she said, surprised at the remorse and angst in his tone.

He didn't look convinced, his face drawn in tight lines. "But if this happened this morning, why didn't you call me and tell me? I would have canceled my meetings to be here for you."

"I know you would have, and I didn't want you to. The only bright spot in this whole day right now, besides being with you, is knowing that those meetings will bring you one step closer to building the new community art center."

He nodded, seeming mollified by her response. "What can I do to help you feel better? I made reservations for us to eat at that new sushi bar, but in light of today's events, we can settle for somewhere quieter. Maybe just takeout if you prefer."

Despite the half pint of ice cream from earlier, her stomach growled at the thought of actual food. Other than toast this morning, she hadn't eaten much. "Takeout sounds great."

"Good, because I'm starved, and if you didn't notice, I have a sweet Mercedes GT Coupe on loan outside, ready to take us wherever we want. So what are you feeling like? Thai? Chinese? Burgers?"

"Definitely Chinese."

"Then Chinese it is."

His chipper, upbeat swing in mood had her mood lifting. Stressing about work any more than she already had was wasted energy. What she wanted was to relax with her boyfriend and eat her weight in Chinese food.

Maybe even play a little Speed with stakes higher than the satisfaction of winning.

She grinned, already feeling the adrenaline rushing through her.

DYLAN MADE small talk as he drove them to the restaurant, careful to keep his voice upbeat and casual even if inside he was racked with guilt and anger over everything that had transpired against Tessa. All because of him.

Tessa being bullied by internet trolls thanks to his ex-girlfriend's social media post. Tessa suspended from a job where she'd worked hard, a job that she could very well lose. And now being stalked by paparazzi. He was afraid to see what another day would bring.

He pulled into a spot not far from the restaurant and took the keys from the ignition, ready to grab the food.

"No, let me get it. I'm less likely to be noticed than you," Tessa said. "Since your arrival at my place seems to have escaped the paparazzi's notice, let's not take any chances."

He looked around. "I don't think anyone followed us. Let me come along at least."

"Not a chance," she said and leaned over to kiss him. "I'm not running the risk. Not today."

She hopped out before he could voice any further argument. Not seeing much choice, Dylan remained in the car, scanning through his phone to pass the time. Even though he usually made a rule of ignoring any social media posts that concerned him, he figured he should at least see what was the current buzz for Tessa's sake.

He flinched as he read the comments from people who had no idea who Tessa was or how amazing she was. People who chose to make cruel and false statements just because she had the gall to date someone they thought should be with someone else.

Damn. No wonder she was upset.

He stared again at the phone, hating the fact he was considering calling Roxie to do whatever he had to so she'd pull her fans and their vitriol back, but not seeing much choice. Before the call could connect, however, some movement to his left caught his attention, and he glanced over, nearly missing the guy who was sitting low in the front seat of the dark sedan, the glint of light from the headlight of a passing car on the camera lens tipping off his hiding spot.

Had to be paparazzi. Probably had been there all along, tailing them in hopes of some primo photo. Up ahead, Tessa came out of the restaurant with the food, unaware of the photographer across the street as she smiled and waved to him.

In a flash, more guys with cameras he hadn't seen before suddenly emerged from the darkness and descended on Tessa, who still hadn't recognized what was about to happen.

Oh, hell.

Dylan disconnected the call and hopped out, ready to mow everyone down if he had to to protect Tessa, public display or not. As he drew near, he could see from the panic and shock in her face she knew the mob was intended for her, and he called out her name.

She stepped back to get away from them. At seeing his approach, the photographers turned their cameras to him, but his attention was only on Tessa, who, in her haste to get away, had misjudged the distance from the curb and was falling backwards. Her shoulder slammed against the asphalt first as her head swung down and landed in a sickening thud. Dylan was still pushing people away as an approaching car swerved in time to keep from hitting her.

"Tessa?" he asked so quietly as he reached her, his voice hoarse as he tried to restrain his terror. He heard someone say, "Call an ambulance" just as Tessa moved her head and opened her eyes, taking a moment to refocus on him.

"Dylan? What happened?"

"You fell." He studied her, looking for any bleeding. "Are you hurt? Tell me where you're hurting."

She seemed dazed as she thought about it. "My shoulder is hurting pretty good. And my head."

He nodded, relieved she was conscious and coherent.

Whatever professionalism had temporarily ceased the photographers' attack disappeared, and the flashing of bulbs from the cameras resumed. Damn. It was a risk, but hell if he was going to let her lie here as those cretins took advantage of the situation to get their shots.

"Tell me if I'm hurting you," he said and slipped his hands under her body and tentatively took her weight in his arms.

She grimaced but didn't say anything. Drawing his

strength, he pulled her up and came to his feet, cradling her. He didn't stop as he made his way back to the car and opened the passenger door, gently setting her down. She stared dazedly ahead as the fury of flashes continued.

Swearing under his breath, he managed to contain his fury as he reached his door and climbed in. "You're going to be okay."

"Of course. Once I get home and lie down, I'll be fine."

"Sure. Right after I take you to the hospital to be checked out."

"It's nothing, Dylan. I'll be fine. Nothing that some ibuprofen and ice won't cure."

"All the same, I'll feel better if the doctors check you over." He glanced in his rearview mirror at the circus he left behind, the bag of takeout spilled all over the sidewalk.

That had been close. A few inches more and her head could have been out on the road, crushed under the wheel of a car.

All because of him.

SPLITTING PAIN EMANATED from the back of her head as Tessa woke up early the next morning. She peered at the clock. Eight thirty. She tried to sit up, flinching as she absently put weight on her right hand.

That's right.

She'd fallen hard, and as a reminder, she had a sprained wrist and the entire right side of her body was bruised and aching. Tentatively, she reached for the bottle of medicine and water, slurping them down before trying to get her bearings.

It was strange to wake up back in her bed in the city, the

whole place empty as her roommates had undoubtedly gone off to work, neither of them aware of the turmoil Tessa had experienced over the past twenty-four hours. It made her feel oddly empty and alone to not be able to share that with them.

Then there was Dylan. After days of newfound joy and happiness basking in his attention, she could sense even before she'd taken the fall that something was off. But his pensiveness had grown as they reached the hospital, and he'd barely been able to hold her gaze. She'd tried to laugh off her fall, told him that she was going to have to invest in protective gear if she was going to date a rock star, but the laughter had been forced.

Her last words to him when he tucked her in bed and kissed her chastely on the forehead were that her fall wasn't his fault, something she'd been sensing he might feel responsible for.

He hadn't responded.

Glancing around her room now, she stopped when she realized that Dylan was still there, sleeping in the chair by her window.

He'd stayed here all night? Watching over her?

As if he sensed her scrutiny, Dylan's eyes opened.

"Hey," she said. "Did you sleep there?"

He raised his arms above his head and stretched before wiping the sleep from his eyes. "I was sitting here most of the time. Sleep was a little harder. I did meet your roommate last night. Quinn, I think? Brown hair and an inquisitive disposition?"

She smiled, flinching slightly at the pain. "That sounds about right. No Anna?"

"She texted you both saying she was staying with Nick. I told Quinn about the accident and assured her that I would stay with you through the night and see that you were okay in the morning. She was kind of torn up that she couldn't stay. I guess she has some trial she's in the middle of, but Anna is going to be here soon."

"How are you holding up?"

"Me? I should be asking you the same. Did you need some pain meds?" he asked, looking her over.

"I just took them. I'm going to be sore for a few days but nothing was broken, no concussion, so I would say that I got away fairly unscathed."

"I wouldn't say unscathed." His expression and tone said he didn't agree with her, and she could see anger in his brown eyes.

"I'll be fine, Dylan. Really. Hey, at least I don't have to worry about asking for more time off from the partners, right? I'm already suspended," she said, trying for humor. But he didn't smile, not even a glimmer of one. "Hey. What's wrong?"

He studied his fingers for a long moment, her unease growing. "I was up all night, all these thoughts running through my head about us."

She swallowed, careful to sound casual as she asked, "What about us?"

He breathed in heavily and let it out before taking a seat on the bed. "I just—I just have been thinking that things have gotten pretty complicated for you since I came back into the picture. With you maybe losing your job, all the public fury wrongly directed your way, and that frenzy of paparazzi who nearly killed you last night?"

"They hardly nearly killed me. My falling was because of my own clumsiness."

His eyes were almost haunted as he shook his head. "It wasn't your fault."

"Well, it certainly wasn't yours," she snapped back, suddenly trying to tamp down the fear that this thing she had just started to embrace was somehow at risk of being pulled away from her.

"Look, Tessa," he said, his voice soft and imploring. "I was wrong to think I could just jump back in your life after all this time, that there wouldn't be consequences. I didn't really see the full picture. Things are always going to be complicated where they concern me. I'll be on the road half the year once this next tour gets going, which means I'll be coming in and out of your life, always bringing with me drama and all that"—he nodded his head outside to what she assumed meant the photographers—"which, if you haven't lost your job already, could jeopardize it all over again. You deserve better than that. You deserve stability, a life not subject to public scrutiny. You deserve a good, happy life with someone who won't...complicate it. Someone like Eric."

Something inside her felt like it was being torn open, and a fury rose up, fury that had been buried these past few years but was only starting to flow to the surface. Of anger and things that were still unsaid between them.

"So what? You're going to leave again? Give up?" she asked, her voice eerily calm despite her unleashed fury. "No discussion? I mean, this involves me, too. Shouldn't I have some say in the matter?"

"That's what we're doing now. And I'm telling you that maybe we should take a step back for a little while. Make sure that this is something you want in your life. Lord knows I have a few things I probably need to sort through, too. Like my dad's death, finding out I have a sister, not to mention this new business venture with Finn and this album I need to write."

183

A lot of excuses. A lot of things that he could deal with if he really wanted to be with her.

The truth was staring at her in the face.

He didn't want her. She was a liability. A drain to his life and schedule.

She couldn't hear any more. It was like before. He was going to leave and there wasn't anything she could do about it.

"Okay. You're right. You've said what you wanted to say. But I can't stay on this ride anymore. We could have had a future. But you're too damned stubborn and scared to see that all over again. You know, I don't need a week or a month or even a year to know that you're not the man I thought you might be. You take care of whatever needs fixing, but I'm not going to be waiting for you when you're done."

He was silent, his face tense as they glared at each other. This was what he wanted, wasn't it? Another reason to disappear permanently? If he'd expected her to plead with him, to sob uncontrollably that everything would be okay, he'd be disappointed. She wasn't that person.

She was going to cry all right, but only after he left.

"I need you to go, Dylan. Just...go." She swallowed a large lump that found its way into her throat.

More seconds passed until she saw the answer in his eyes. The resignation that hung from his broad shoulders as he reached his feet. Suddenly, an overwhelming sense of panic swept over her. A panic that came when you were about to lose someone who meant the entire world to you and there wasn't a thing you could do about it.

She'd had it when she heard about her mom.

She'd had it when Dylan walked away ten years ago.

And she was having it now.

Unwittingly, she put her hand to her mouth, biting back the impulse to ask him to stay, to beg him not to go even though she'd just said the opposite moments before. Her heart ached and her breathing became more and more difficult as she watched him head to the door, pausing briefly.

Then he was gone, the sound of the front door shutting a minute later echoing through the empty place.

He'd left her again. She'd let it happen all over again.

Why had she given him another chance? Opening herself up to this kind of pain wasn't worst the risk.

Love wasn't worth the risk.

THIRTEEN

"DYLAN! COME JOIN US."

Dylan glanced over to the table in the hotel bar, where he spotted Roxie and a handful of her band and crew. He'd been sitting here for the past half hour nursing the same drink as he mulled over the train wreck he'd made of his life and Tessa's over the past week.

He shook his head, holding up his drink as if to say cheers before returning to his thoughts. He wasn't in any mood for company. He hadn't been ever since he left Tessa's place Wednesday morning and arrived here in LA, especially not the company of one Roxie Mann, who, in exchange for Dylan's agreeing to perform in Saturday night's concert, had deleted her previous Instagram post and posted a new one that—if not an outright apology—got her fans talking about something other than him and Tessa.

It didn't mean that it was water under the bridge for Dylan. But he was here in LA, practicing for his performance and hiding out from the censure he was sure to receive from his aunt and the entire Montenegro clan the moment he returned to Blossom Falls. Deservedly. He'd promised them he would keep Tessa safe. And he'd failed.

It was also why he hadn't returned Jasper's emails about finalizing the sale of the Wallace home, since now that he and Tessa were through, he wasn't sure if moving next door to her family home was a good idea for either of them.

"Here. Compliments of your friends," the bartender said and set a shot of tequila in front of him.

Unwanted company or not didn't mean he couldn't enjoy a free drink. He tossed it back.

"Care for some company?"

Roxie Mann's deep, sultry voice was unmistakable, and Dylan didn't bother to glance over to her as she slid into the barstool next to him.

"Not really, Rox. Kind of could use some time to myself," he said, careful to keep his tone neutral so she wouldn't hear his anger and frustration over the pain she'd caused Tessa in the previous days.

"Drinking alone? You once told me that was the clearest sign of a man who shouldn't be left alone.

That sounded like something he might have said. Before he knew the sanctuary that self-imposed exile could provide someone.

She tried again. "You know, maybe talking about it will help you figure out whatever's bothering you."

He glanced over to see that there was real concern in her light blue eyes. "Talking isn't going to help."

"Okay. Then let me just sit with you for a spell. We don't have to talk."

It was a free country. He couldn't really stop her from sitting anywhere, wanted or not. "Do what you want."

"Does this have something to do what that girl you were flaunting the other day?"

Flaunting? He wouldn't even bother to argue that ludicrous statement. But the rest... "That 'girl' is a bright, kind-hearted attorney who is currently suspended from her job thanks to the unnecessary attention you rained down on her with that post."

"I'm going to take that as a yes." She studied him. "You're not kidding, are you? You're really upset about that. You know me. I don't mean anything by my posts. It's just feeding the social media mob, keeping them appeased. You've never cared about what I said about you before."

"That was because I knew it came with the territory. But Tessa? She has nothing to do with that world, and she had nothing to do with what happened between you and me, and you knew that."

"Your girlfriend has got to get a tougher skin if she's going to be a part of your world. You of all people should know that."

"Tessa is tougher than anyone I know. That's not the point. You posted that to be vindictive. To punish me for not playing your games."

"I posted that because it was good publicity." She stopped herself from whatever she was going to say next and took a drink. "Look. We can argue this point all night. But that's not what I came over here to do. I just wanted to make sure you're okay and to thank you for coming out to do the show."

"You didn't give me much choice."

"You really think I'm that awful, huh? I'm sorry that I hurt your girlfriend, and maybe you have a small point in that I posted that as a gut reaction to seeing you two in that photo, clearly so happy together. I mean, we only just broke up."

"Four months ago because you were cheating on me. What did you expect?"

"I may have slept with someone else, but you and I both know that you left the relationship long before that. Don't play the martyr. You never were as invested in our relationship as you were your career. I was merely someone you were spending time with. Your head—your heart—was always somewhere else."

It took him by surprise that she felt that way. "That's not true. We had a good thing for a while."

"Oh, sure. We had fun. But in the two years we were together, I was never able to reach you—reach the real you, you know what I mean? You never let me in. Hell, I didn't even know you grew up in that tiny town of Flower Falls until the photo of you went viral."

"Blossom Falls."

"Wherever. And what about me? Do you know anything about me? What's my brother's name?"

He drew a blank. "Mark?"

She appeared bemused. "I don't have a brother. And you might have known that if you ever really got to know me. I only wish I would have realized that you were still in love with your old girlfriend so I wouldn't have spent so much time wondering what was wrong with me."

There were so many things she'd said in the statement he didn't know where to start except to clarify one thing. "Tessa and I never dated. She was my best friend's little sister. That's all."

"Sure, whatever you say."

"Roxie," someone called from their table. "Grab us another round."

He waited a moment as she delivered the order to the bartender, who had, by the way he quickly materialized in front of them, been waiting for the opportunity to serve her again. She had that effect on people. Just not him, not anymore.

"Rox," he said when they were alone again. "For the record? Nothing was ever wrong with you. You were everything that I should have wanted. Beautiful, talented, charming, maybe a tad dramatic at times." She feigned an outraged expression before nodding in agreement. "But the reason we didn't work was never you."

"Great. The whole *it's not you it's me* spiel." Only she was smiling as she said it. "It's okay. I've seen the writing on the wall and I'm moving on. I only wish we'd talked more honestly before now."

"Me, too," he said in all sincerity. Because she had a point. He hadn't ever fully been committed to her, and he could see that now, which wasn't fair to her.

"Well, whatever reason you're here drinking alone, I hope you can figure your way out of it, because I saw something in the way you looked at her that I never saw when you looked at me, something I would have given anything for."

He raised a brow in disbelief. "Anything?"

She smiled. "Okay, maybe not anything. But then again, had you looked at me like that, maybe I would have. She's a lucky girl."

The bartender returned with her order, asking if she needed any assistance carrying it out.

"I've got it, thanks." She looked back at Dylan. "For whatever reason you're here, I won't deny that I'm looking forward to having you part of Saturday's show. But I also won't hold it against you if you decide you've got somewhere else to be."

"Not anymore. I'll see you then."

She stood, smoothing out her leather pants over her svelte frame for a moment before grabbing the drink. "If you change your mind and want some company, come and join us. Drinking alone isn't good for anyone."

"Thanks, Roxie. Good night."

With a last smile and flip of her blond hair, she returned to her party, leaving him alone to consider her words. He looked around the place, noticing the guy at the end heavy into his third, maybe fourth drink. Roxie was right. He wasn't going to find any solutions to his problems at the bar.

He needed to write. Needed to put his fingers on his guitar strings, his words to the page, and get whatever was bothering him out in the only way he knew how until he no longer felt this deep anguish of knowing he'd walked out on the best thing in his life. Again.

TESSA STOOD outside the conference room, where the partners had asked her to wait as they finished up their meeting early Friday morning. It had already been nine minutes since she'd arrived, and the dread that had been building was reaching a level that was going to send her climbing the walls soon.

Her hand went to her pocket, where her phone was sitting in the silent mode.

She fought the urge to look at it again. To stare at the photo of Dylan and Roxie in a hotel bar that was circulating on all the morning talk shows, that had trended on Twitter for almost two full hours, and that had torn to shreds the final pieces of her heart. Because as much as it hurt, it was exactly what she needed to reinforce the fact that things were definitely over with Dylan. He'd broken her heart for the last time.

The door opened and one of the partners beckoned her inside.

Taking a shaky breath, she walked in and took a seat again at the table as directed.

As directed.

Just like she'd been doing since she first stepped foot in this firm. She'd been obedient, hardworking, diligent... pretty much a lackey. Something she could take to a point. She'd started as a lowly first year here right after law school. One of many cogs in the wheel. But over time, she should have earned some respect. Someone should have realized that she took her job seriously and would never do anything to jeopardize it or the firm's reputation.

And yet here she was.

Ted started talking, thanking her for her patience over the past couple days as the investigation proceeded. But she barely heard him, caught up in her own thoughts.

What had she been doing it all for? Why had she allowed herself to become a doormat? Was it because it brought her happiness? Self-respect? Job satisfaction? Sure, she felt a sense of satisfaction when they neared the end of a project, but the moment it was done, another one was waiting. More contracts to be negotiated, more leases to research, documents to sign.

She hated her job.

There it was. Plain and simple.

But she'd been happy to bury herself in her work, bury herself in monotonous things so she didn't have to think about how sad and empty her life had become. Aside from her friends, she had nothing to look forward to in her days. She'd dated, but more to kill the time than to look for anything really meaningful. Killing the time in the hopes of burying her feelings for that one guy who would always be a dream. She could see that now.

But it was over. Finito.

And she didn't know if she wanted to just kill time anymore. She wanted to do something more meaningful. Help people, actual people with their everyday problems. Things that she could do as an associate at a family law practice. It didn't have to be Blossom Falls. It could be here in the city or anywhere, really.

She realized that everyone was staring at her, waiting for her to respond to whatever question had been put to her.

The nerves she felt were gone. Her heart was still cold and sad and would be for a long time, but she at least finally realized where and what she wanted to do.

And she couldn't wait to tell them exactly that.

She smiled.

Tessa grabbed the scouring brush Saturday afternoon and got to work on the farmhouse's kitchen sink that, in the few short days since she'd left, had managed to build up a nice grayish pallor from grease and dirt. It also served as a great distraction from the shambles what was currently her life. By the end of the weekend, everyone would need sunglasses from the shine she'd have on every surface.

But she had her entire future to work out, particularly what she was going to do now that she was unemployed. For a brief moment, when she'd seen the Blossom Falls sign as she drove into town, she'd felt a sense of belonging, of yearning that this was where she was meant to be, a sentiment that lasted until the moment she passed the turnoff that would take her to the Wallace place—or rather, Dylan's place. Because how could she face every day knowing there was a possibility of seeing him?

No, she couldn't open herself to that kind of pain. But there were other towns. Santa Rosa had some good prospects. But for now, she had some time.

The only drawback in her decision to leave her job and the city behind her was the thought of leaving her two friends and their cozy little home. They'd been understanding but disappointed, even though they all knew that their situation was bound to end soon, what with Quinn getting married in the spring and Anna probably getting engaged herself.

It was time.

"Honey, you don't have to do that," her dad said when he caught sight of her as he walked into the kitchen.

"I don't mind. It's relaxing," she said as she scoured a particularly troublesome spot that, come to think of it, had been there for at least ten years. Not for long.

"Is this about you quitting your job? Because you know that you are welcome to stay here for as long as you need until you find something else."

She blew a strand of hair from her face. "Thanks, Dad. That means a lot. But no, I'm okay with that decision. And I have some savings, not a lot, but enough to tide me over for a little while."

"I see." He took a seat on a barstool. "You know, honey, I may not have a lot of experience in the dating world, but I can tell that something seems to be going on with you and Dylan. Care to tell me about it?"

She scrubbed harder at the smudge. It...wasn't... coming...out. "Not really much to say, Dad. Dylan did what he does best and ran the moment things got complicated."

"What happened?" he asked.

She bit her lip, debating whether to embroil her dad in her personal life like this. But he had perspective that her friends didn't have in knowing both her and Dylan, and it was that perspective she needed now. Even if to make her feel better about things.

So she told him. Told him about the pictures on Instagram, the public reaction, the events the other night with the paparazzi, and finally the resigned look on Dylan's face as he threw in the towel and decided that fighting for her wasn't worth it.

Her dad took a while to process the information before finally speaking. "Sounds to me like he just had a gut response. Wanted to protect you is all. Have you tried to talk with him since? Reasoned with him? Because whatever was said, it doesn't undo the way he feels about you. The way he looks at you every time he sees you just as you look when you see him."

"There's not anything more for us to say to each other, Dad. I can't keep playing this game with him where he is in and then he's out. It hurts too much. From now on, I'm out. From all of it. You've had the right idea all these years. Not putting your heart out there just to have it crushed when the inevitable happens and life takes it all away."

"Now wait a minute. I don't know what you mean by life taking happiness and love away. All of that is out there for you, with or without Dylan, and I've been realizing that it's also out there for me. I wasn't exactly setting a good example to you and the boys these past few years about moving on with life. I was crushed and heartbroken and didn't think I could go on without your mother, and I wallowed for too long in my pain. But this accident was a wake-up call to how much of a rut I've gotten in and how much I've let myself become a burden to you kids."

"Dad, you will never be a burden to us. We love you and we love being there to help you, especially when you needed us most. You don't have to go dating all these women just because you don't want to be alone. We'll always be here for you."

He chuckled. "There are a lot of reasons for me to finally get out there, honey. It's time. Sticking around here, not opening myself to new relationships only hurts me in the end. Sure, there's a risk to getting involved with anyone, developing feelings that may never be returned. But it's worth it. Do you think I would exchange one minute of the time I had with your mom to save myself any of the pain I've had at her loss? Never. Every minute with her was worth it all. And you'll find that out, too, once you put yourself on the line."

"I put myself on the line," she said, feeling defensive. "I date all the time."

"Like that Eric? The guy whose call you avoided until he came here, just to get your attention?"

"Eric was different. He and I just...didn't connect."

"And what about all the other guys? Can you honestly tell me you've really opened yourself up to having a relationship with any of them? To loving them with every fiber of your being like I loved your mom?"

She wanted to say yes, even if just to keep up the pretense for his sake. But she knew he was right on some level. Loving someone with all your heart and soul only left you open to pain, something she couldn't risk.

"Tessa, when you're lucky enough to find that person who you love more than anything, who makes your heart light and happy and alive, then you're truly blessed. Just as I was blessed, and I'm still blessed because I have all of you guys in my life."

She blinked back tears at the emotion she heard in her dad's voice. A pang of guilt hit her because, as mature as she liked to think she was, over the past few days, she had resented him and his ease of getting back into the dating world, as if it were some sort of betrayal to her mom.

She wiped her hands on a towel and walked over to him, wrapping her arms around him. "I am happy that you're out there again. I don't want you to be alone in this old house without anyone to take care of you. Anyone to love you. I hope you can find someone who will make you happy again."

"Thanks, sweetie. I hope we can both find someone who will make us happy again. But think about it. If Dylan is who makes you happy, maybe you should tell him that. Let him know you're of stronger stock than he's credited you for. Let him know you're all in."

She wasn't so sure about that, not right now, not after seeing the confirmation that, after all his protestations that things were over with Roxie, he'd decided to join her in tonight's concert. And she'd seen the photo of the two of them at that bar. He didn't seem to be as resistant to her charms as he'd pretended.

But she wasn't going to think about Dylan. Not anymore. She had to move on, and she had to admit, the sadness that hung over her seemed to have lifted. Opportunities were all around her, she just had to see them.

"Now," he continued and leaned back, taking his time to look her over. "If you're still of a mind to get some cleaning done to settle your thoughts, maybe you can work on the area under the stairs. Lord knows how much we could stand to free up some of the space." He touched her cheek before slipping a little stiffly from the barstool. "In the meantime, I'm going to go see if your brother needs any help. Don't worry, I'll be careful."

She smiled and watched as he strolled out the door, his limp barely noticeable. She glanced at the sink. It practically glistened. Well, she might as well keep herself busy until tonight's farewell party for Claudia and the art studio.

It took her a minute to unload some of the furniture blocking access into the small storage area under the stairs to actually get to the things she knew, the moment she saw them, that her dad had wanted her to find.

He was wiser than she'd given him credit for.

Twenty minutes later, she stood in front of her art easel that now rested in its old spot in the family room, right by the large window that let in the most light. She'd found not one but three canvasses still untouched and blank and ready to tell a story, as well as the rest of her brushes and oil paints. The paints were going to need replacing, the oil and pigment separated, but she'd swirled the colors she needed enough that it would do for now.

She didn't even have to think about what she wanted to paint. It was like opening that door had unleashed all the pictures she'd already framed in her mind all these years, and she couldn't wait to get started.

FOURTEEN

"Someone's here for you, Mr. Charles," the person at the front desk announced.

Dylan had been working on his music the past few hours and had almost not bothered to take the call, knowing that he had to be leaving soon if he wanted to arrive early to the arena for tonight's show.

It wasn't unusual for a few rabid fans to have dug up his location in the hopes of meeting him, but he'd stayed at this hotel a few times in the past and they were professional. They screened everyone who attempted to get through.

"Can you see what they want? I've got to leave in a few minutes."

There was a pause. "I usually would, sir, but the young lady seems fairly insistent that she needs to see you. I think you're going to want her to come up." All thoughts immediately rushed to Tessa. She'd come here to make him see reason, to tell him that they would figure out a way to work through the publicity and the reporters and all the negative attention that came with dating him and to tell him he was an idiot for doubting that. Before his thoughts could go further astray, the guy clarified, "She says she's your sister."

Elle? His hand went to his head, rubbing the worry lines he was quickly getting since having her in his life. "All right. Send her up."

A few minutes later, there was a slight knock on the door. He opened it, sighing wearily. "Does your mom know you're here?"

"What do you think?" Elle asked and slipped by him, her backpack bumping him as she passed.

"Come right in," he said, bemused. "Is there any particular reason you once again risked your life in coming all the way out here to see me? And how on earth did you even know where I'm staying?"

"Duh. Remember we set up that *Find My Friends* app last weekend when Tessa and I lost you at the festival? I can see you wherever you are."

He'd forgotten about that, and how he'd accepted her request to be friends, not exactly realizing what he was signing on for. She could see where he was...always? He'd have to reconsider that one. "All right. So you found me, but how did you get here?"

"I kind of borrowed some of that money you sent my mom and bought an airline ticket."

His mind raced as he considered what she said. "They just let you on the plane, no questions asked?"

"I had all the forms filled out ahead of time," she said a little too proudly. "And mom's signature isn't that hard to copy."

"You forged your mom's signature? And they didn't ask any questions, require a guardian to at least see you off?"

"I paid the Uber driver extra to walk me to the gate just in case, but they didn't need to see him."

He sat down, his hands wrapped around his head. The risk she took was going to kill him just as surely as her mom was going to kill her. "Okay. So you're here. Now what was so important you had to come to see me?"

"To tell you how much of a jerk you are." Why did that sound familiar? "I can't believe you are back with that stupid Roxie Mann and not with Tessa. And then you go and make plans to go get pancakes with me and then break them. Just so you can sing at some stupid concert."

"Whoa, whoa, whoa. I'm not back together with anyone. Where did you get that idea?"

"Because you're playing in her show and it's all anyone can talk about, how you two had to have made up. For a public person, you would think you'd know your way around social media by now."

This kid. "I'm not back with Roxie. As to the pancakes... I'm sorry. I forgot, and I'll make it up to you, but that's no reason to do what you just did. What am I going to do with you? I'm leaving to get ready for the show in a few minutes. I can't just leave you here alone."

"Why not? I'm almost thirteen. I can watch TV and do some homework and I won't cause any trouble. And if I need something, I can call someone from the front desk to help me," she said in a pleading tone.

"That's up to your mom, not me." The problem was, it was probably the only solution, since he couldn't very well take her to the show without any supervision, let alone leave her to roam backstage. Too much could happen. Her mom was going to have to be okay with it since he couldn't possibly get her to the airport and back on a flight before he had to be on stage. That didn't mean he was looking forward to breaking the news to Lana about her daughter's latest adventure.

"And what about Tessa? I really liked her. Don't you like her anymore? She's so nice and funny, and I was really hoping that she might even be my sister someday. Because you two were so...so perfect."

There was a lump forming in his throat that he swallowed past. "Wish it were that easy. Let's just say that sometimes things are complicated, and loving someone doesn't make those complications go away."

"But you're not with Roxie Mann?"

"Nope. Look, Elle. I really don't have time for the third degree. You being here has really put me in a bind, and I need to go call your mom and figure out what we're going to do with you."

Her eyes widened at his sharp tone, and he could see that he'd hurt her feelings. But he didn't have time for this or to babysit her, either.

"Wait here while I call your mom, please. Watch TV if you want," he said, trying to soften his tone.

Five minutes later, he came out to find Elle on the couch, a purple photo album open on her lap. "Looks like your mom is resigned to having you stick around here, but first thing in the morning, you're on a flight back home."

"Okay. But maybe after pancakes?"

She certainly had a one-track mind. "We'll see. If you can stay out of trouble before I get back." He came over and took a seat, his conversation with Lana having taken it out of him. He glanced over to her book. "What have you got there?"

"Something Mom put together for me since I was a baby. I thought you might like to see it."

He glanced at his watch, knowing he should leave but also wanting to make sure they were on level ground after his earlier behavior. Five minutes. He could give her five minutes. "All right. Show me."

She beamed at him before flipping the pages back to the beginning of the book. "This is me in Mom's stomach. She said that I gave her terrible morning sickness and a lifelong aversion to eggs."

The picture was of Lana looking for all the world like she was the luckiest person on earth even though she could barely be eighteen at the time. Elle turned the page, showing off photos of herself as a baby with a bright shock of red hair at the top of her head even then.

His stomach dropped a little when she got to the picture of his old man, this time holding the squirming baby girl as Lana looked on. "Mom said he loved to count my toes and fingers, amazed at how small they were."

"Do you remember him at all?"

"A little, I think. He was on the road a lot. I remember he liked to pretend he was going to throw me in the tub because my hair was on fire, which I thought was the funniest thing. I remember he liked to play the guitar a lot, kind of like you do, and he'd play all sorts of silly songs. He would also talk about you and how you really were something and how proud he was of you."

Dylan didn't have a response. Wasn't sure if he could really believe that his old man had given him a second thought the moment after he walked out of his life. But this was Elle. She wouldn't make this up.

He studied the pages in front of him more closely. What he saw was a man who seemed more defeated and sadder than he had in his earlier pictures, like the one his mom had kept. Definitely a man who might have had more than a few regrets.

On the pages before him, he could see that indeed the

old man was present physically and emotionally in Elle's young life. But it was when Elle turned around six that the happy family disappeared, and Lana was probably feeling as alone as his mom had. He studied her. Sure, she looked a little sad early on, but most of the moments she still looked lovingly at her daughter, all her hopes and dreams she had for her child still in her eyes.

He thought of the flimsy box his aunt had sent home with him the other night, filled with bits of a life he had before he came to Blossom Falls. A few rare photos, some odds and ends. Most of Dylan's memories, however, weren't found in the contents of the box. His memories he carried with him. Memories of a lonely existence before he'd come to Blossom Falls with a woman who just couldn't find enough reason to join the living. Not even for him. She'd let her grief consume her.

All the anger and resentment Dylan had over the years over what he'd never had always focused on his dad. He'd never known fully until this moment how much anger he had for his mom, too.

She didn't have to give up when Brick Jamison had walked out of their lives. Lana had struggled as a single mom and not given up or let herself be controlled by self-pity and anger. She had a daughter to raise, and that's what she focused on. And then there was Tessa's dad, who had lost the love of his life and he hadn't emotionally abandoned his children.

People moved on. But his mom hadn't. Or couldn't. He'd blamed himself for that, thinking if he'd been a better kid, better student, she'd snap out of it. But no amount of A's or B's or help around the house made a difference.

Only Dylan wasn't to blame for that.

The truth was that his mom hadn't been strong enough.

Maybe she hadn't had anyone who believed in her enough growing up. Maybe she hadn't had the support of friends and family that he eventually had when he moved to Blossom Falls. He'd never know.

And just like that, his pent-up anger slipped away. He could forgive her her weakness, forgive her for abandoning him, forgive her because, even through it all, he still loved her. Just as now he could forgive the weaknesses of an old man who didn't know what a good life he could have had had he been present.

Dylan turned the pages until he got to one of him and Elle. A selfie from that first time they'd played games at the farm. On the next page was one of him, Elle, and Tessa at the Harvest Festival. Tessa, smiling so openly with all the love and passion she could offer someone shining there in her eyes.

This was a woman who was strong. This was a woman who had born the loss of her mother and had gone on. Who'd been subjected to the teasing and roughhousing of growing up the only girl with five boys and learned to give as good as she got. Who somehow had found room in her heart for him when he first appeared on their front porch and had only made more room for him as the years went by. Who'd loved him even when he didn't want to be loved or feel worthy of love. Who'd been put through hell when he walked out on her ten years ago and had still gone on to accomplish so much. Who had, through her pain and terror of letting him back in, given him another chance.

She wasn't like his mom. Tessa could overcome the trials and tribulations that came with being in love with someone like him. And he'd pushed her away, been willing to walk away to save her. Little had he known that he was the one to be saved. By her. By her love.

He didn't know how long he just sat there, lost in his thoughts, until Elle finally punched him in the shoulder to get his attention. "Aren't you going to be late for your concert?"

It took him a moment to answer as he thought over his decision, trying to figure out how he'd get it done. "No. I'm not going to be late, because I'm not going. In fact, you and I have other plans. But we need to get a move on if we're going to get to the airport before the evening flight leaves."

"You're taking me home?" She looked so disappointed and heartbroken. "You're that mad at me?"

He smiled. "Not in the least. But I'm going to need your help with a pretty big mission. I'll explain it to you on the way. Come on."

FOR MID-OCTOBER, the weather was unseasonably warm, and with the sun still perched above the horizon, it could almost have passed as a late-summer evening for Tessa as she, Quinn, and Anna reached the town square, the venue for tonight's party. It had been a surprise when, an hour before, she'd opened the door to find her best friends standing there with smiles on their faces, having canceled all their plans to make sure she was settled in and had all the support she needed during this time.

She was going to miss them, but this was a reminder that no matter what happened, they'd always be a part of each other's lives.

"Who'd have thought our own sweet, easygoing Tessa was such a woman of mystery," Anna said, linking her arm through hers as they passed a couple of fired-up grills where the sizzling scent of savory burgers and hot dogs filled the air. "First we find out you and one Dylan Charles not only grew up together but shared a secret romance, and then we discover that you're an incredibly talented artist. Who are you?"

Tessa laughed. It had been hard to hide the painting she'd been working on when they arrived, and they'd been raving about it ever since. She'd surprised herself with how easy it had been to return to her love, and to actually see that her paint strokes, although a little less practiced, still did the image in her mind justice.

She'd started painting a picture of her mom after she died, but then Dylan and that heartbreak got in the way and she'd never finished it. Which was why it was the image that compelled her the most to start again. To give life to the curves in the woman's face, the arch of her brow, the warmth in those eyes.

"It really was beautiful, what you've done so far," Quinn added. "Does this mean that you're going to take a break from practicing law? Pursue your art instead for a little while? Because if you're serious, I know James and his family are contributors to several major art foundations and galleries and could arrange some meetings if you wanted."

"That's sweet. But for now, I'm going to take things day by day. There's no reason to rush into anything." Up ahead, Tessa saw Claudia talking to a couple of people. "Actually, I need to go say hello to someone. Go try the custard and apple cider doughnuts and I'll join you guys in a minute."

Seeing her arrival, Claudia stepped away from her friends, grabbing Tessa for a quick hug before stepping back. "I'm thrilled you could make it after all, Tessa. This isn't quite the ending you wanted, but I want you to know how pleased I am with the result."

"I'm glad then," Tessa said. "You made such a difference

in my life when I needed it the most. Probably did for a lot of people if the size of this crowd is any indication."

"Thank you, my dear. Actually, I have something for you. Come with me," she said and led Tessa over to a table, where she dug underneath the tablecloth and brought out a couple of canvasses. "I wanted you to have these," she said and presented them to Tessa.

They were her old paintings. One she recognized as having hung up in the art studio; the other she hadn't seen in years, still waiting to be finished. It was precisely this painting that she'd decided to recreate this afternoon.

"I almost wanted to keep them both for myself," Claudia continued. "I've enjoyed looking at them over the years. But I think it's time they were returned to you. Maybe they'll even inspire you to pick up a brush again?" she asked almost hopefully.

Tessa was still staring at the second canvas. It was one she'd done right after her mom died. She'd meant to capture everything that her mom had meant to her, something that Claudia had encouraged her to do in those weeks when she felt so lost and alone. She'd only been eighteen at the time, but she could see on the lines of the canvas everything her mom had meant to her in every brushstroke, every choice in color, and in every tear that she remembered shedding as she'd worked on it. It was beautiful. And being able to express that pain through her painting had been a cathartic release.

Even then, at such a young age, she could admit that she'd had talent.

And now? she wondered. Maybe there was room for both. A little whimsy, a little bit of dreaming, mixed with the practicality of life and her law practice, wherever she ended up.

She smiled as she looked up at Claudia again. "Who knows? Maybe I will."

"Tessa!" someone shouted across the square, and Tessa looked up to see Elle racing across the grass toward her. At her heels at a slower, more leisurely rate was another figure, a figure who still could send her heart pouncing right out of her chest.

She felt Claudia pat her on the arm before moving away, leaving her alone to face the approaching Jamisons.

"Tessa, Tessa, I hoped we'd find you," Elle said, wrapping her arms around her.

Tessa tried to find a smile as she hugged her back, all too aware of the hulking man still bearing down on her. He shouldn't be here. He wasn't supposed to be here. By all accounts, he was supposed to be in LA preparing to perform with Roxie Mann. Something that had served to remind her of how different their lives were and why, although the way things ended had been tough, the decision was right.

Only he wasn't in LA. He was here.

She wasn't ready to face him. Wasn't yet strong enough to be sure she wouldn't crumple before him and beg him to have her back. But there was no escape from those eyes. So she would have to wait for the impact. And stay strong.

"Hi," he said.

"Hi," she managed to say despite the tightness in her lungs.

"Hey, Dylan, is it okay if I grab a hot dog?" Elle asked. "The last thing I ate was those cookies on the plane and I'm super hungry."

"Of course, kiddo. Maybe you can grab me one. Maybe a soda, too," he called as she ran over to join the line.

Just act natural, Tessa. You were bound to run into him

at some point. "I'm surprised to see you here. Aren't you supposed to be playing in a concert in LA?"

"I was. But then Elle knocked on my door."

Tessa gasped. "She didn't."

"She most certainly did. However, it's been hard for me to stay mad at her considering she helped me see a few things that I couldn't before."

"Her mom knows her whereabouts, I take it?"

"Oh, yeah. And if I were Elle, I'd be enjoying my last day of freedom."

Tessa smiled wryly and studied his face, looking for any signs of the stress that she'd worn on her own face these past long days. "She's pretty stubborn, I guess. Can't keep her in one place." *Must be genetic.* "You're cutting it kind of close, wouldn't you say, if you plan on still flying back to LA in time for the concert."

"I'm not playing in the concert. Not anymore."

She raised a brow. "And does Roxie know this?"

"She does. I called her on the way out here. But don't worry. We've reached an understanding."

And like that, it felt like someone was crushing her heart in their hand. Okay, Dylan was crushing it. "Congratulations. I'm happy for you two," she managed to choke out.

"Congratula—? No. You don't understand. Sure, initially she wanted to hurt us, and I may have agreed to play in exchange for her changing the narrative on the story about us. Leaving you out of it. But we've talked since then and both of us are on the same page. We were never a good fit. Not when I've always been in love with you."

Oof. He couldn't say those kinds of things to her. He just couldn't. It hurt too much.

She shook her head and walked away, aware of him

following anyhow. "No. No. You can't come here and say that kind of stuff to me. Not anymore, Dylan."

He reached out to try and take her hand, but she pulled it away. "Hey. Stop. Please, Tessa. Let me say this to you, and then if you still want me to leave, I will."

She raised her head to the sky, saying a quick prayer that she'd have the fortitude to stay strong, not let him see her cry. She stopped and crossed her arms over her chest. "Five minutes."

"Fair enough." He ran his hand through his hair, as if trying to find the right words to start. "You knew a little of what my life was like before I came to Blossom Falls. Of my mom, who let the ravages of drugs and drinking take hold of her life after my dad left, until it ultimately consumed her. I'd vowed never to let another person have such power over my own life—or, maybe more importantly, never to have such power in anyone else's life. To never be the one responsible for their pain and suffering, as my dad had been to Mom, to Lana, and who knows how many other women. You see, all those years, I'd put the blame on him. On why my life had been so crappy. Then I came here and met this little, spunky nine-year-old girl who saw someone better than I thought I was. You looked at me and knew I was worth loving. Worth waiting for."

She remembered him that first day, sitting on the top porch step as he watched everyone play, trying to pretend he didn't want to join them, to be part of the fun. But she could also see the yearning in those eyes and she'd decided then that she'd make sure he felt wanted. How little she knew then how those feelings would bloom so big and full in her heart the longer she knew him. Pinching the inside of her hand, she willed herself not to cry or tear up, to let him know how much his words already were affecting her.

"It wasn't that I was afraid of loving you, or what that could mean to my future. It was only because I loved you so much that I didn't want to see you putting your life and dreams on hold. Like my mom did all those years ago for my dad until she lost her way. You deserved better. And then the other night, you were hurting from all the crap coming down on you because of me, and I figured once again, you deserved better. A better life. One that wouldn't rip you apart and take everything away from you that you deserve."

Idiot. She didn't blame him for what had happened. He couldn't help what had happened. But he could help how he'd reacted. Not believing they could work through it together. That they wouldn't be strong enough.

"It took Elle arriving this evening to remind me of how strong and brave you are. How you have a heart so full of love and compassion that you would never end up like my mom. She made her choices, let her grief consume her life. But she isn't you. I shouldn't have let you go. I should have seen that, together, we could take on anything. Be each other's support."

She could have told him that, had he given her the chance. But he hadn't. He'd just...left.

"Please, Tessa. Tell me that I haven't blown it. Because I know that if you say yes, our life together will be amazing. Happy. Filled with ups and downs, no doubt. But all the same, it will be blessed."

Blessed. The word resonated with what her dad had said earlier.

Another breeze picked up, leaving her hair crossing her face, and she took the moment to clear it away, trying to find words as Dylan stood there expectantly. Waiting for forgiveness.

Something that she was surprised to find she was ready to give.

"I love you, Tessa Montenegro," he continued, unaware of the restraint she was showing in not rushing into his arms. "Your love is the only thing that's worth having in this world, and I'll do anything to earn that again. You don't have to answer right now. If it's time you need, I'll give it to you. But I'm going to show you every day that I'm here and in this thing, even if you keep sending me away. I'm not leaving you, not again."

She blinked through the tears that threatened to fall, but she willed them back. Just for a few minutes more. Until she got through this, said what she needed to say.

"You were wrong to walk out on me the other day," she said, her voice stronger than she expected. "But I have to admit, I was wrong, too. I should have stopped you. I could have insisted that you were stuck with me no matter what happened. But I didn't. I held back, letting my own fear of being hurt again stop me from taking what I should have. I saw what loving and losing my mom had done to my dad, and when you left me that first time, I retreated into myself, deciding I would never let myself feel that way about anyone again. But I was wrong. Dad made me see that. I know that every minute we have together will be worth it. No matter how this ends."

His face was incredulous, and he stepped forward, his arms ready to grab her, but stopped. "Are you saying what I think you're saying? That...you forgive me?"

She laughed. "I'm saying that we're going to have to work so that old habits don't creep in and get in the way of what we want. And yes, I forgive you as long as you forgive me, too. Because you're right. I've loved you, Dylan Jamison, for what feels like my entire life. And I want to spend each day of the rest of my life showing you how much I love you. You're stuck with me."

In an instant, she was crushed up against him, his arms holding her so tight, as if he was afraid that she might slip away, a sentiment she shared. Over his shoulders, she could see the smiling faces of her friends watching them, a few people cheering them on, a few others with their phones capturing the moment.

But if it came with the territory of loving Dylan, of being part of his life, she could accept it.

His eyes shined warmly as he stared at her, making her almost blush with the promise held in their brown depths. "I can't imagine any other person I'd rather be stuck with."

Then he kissed her, a soft, magical kiss that was made more so by the fact that she knew in her heart this was a forever kiss.

A forever love.

EPILOGUE

ONE MONTH LATER

"I CAN'T BELIEVE you're leaving. That I'm not going to be able to walk into the kitchen to the heavenly smell of your Sunday cinnamon rolls," Anna said and came to hug Tessa.

"I can't believe I'm not going to have someone around to make fun of Anna when she heads out to run a marathon every morning," Quinn said and joined the hug.

Tessa swallowed against the tears that threatened to fall, but she'd promised herself she wouldn't do that today. Not when she had so much to look forward to waiting for her in Blossom Falls. Dylan, the art center where she would not only be heading it up but teaching art. She even had a new job as Jasper's partner in his law practice. But that didn't make saying good-bye to her best friends and roommates any easier. And the tears fell.

"It's not like I won't see you guys tomorrow when you come out to the farm for Thanksgiving. Just like old times," Tessa said, wiping her tears away. "And you're forgetting that I'm less than an hour's drive away. Less on James's new helicopter."

"True," Quinn said, finally stepping back, wiping her own tears away. "But it won't be the same."

It wouldn't, but this moment was inevitable and they all knew it.

"Look at it as fortuitous timing, what with your sister needing a place to crash for the next few months. My leaving saves her the back pain of the couch."

Dylan walked in, ready to collect the last box remaining on the floor. He laughed when he saw their expressions. "You'd think that Tessa was moving to Siberia instead of Blossom Falls. A town that I shouldn't have to remind you is only an hour away. I promise, I'll take good care of her."

The women still looked skeptically at him. Tessa bit her lip to stop the laughter that threatened. A month ago, her friends had practically idolized the rock star and would have vied for the position of biggest fan, but since the whole breakup, they'd been more careful and reserved in their judgment, even though they seemed to finally be warming up to him now that they could see how happy she was.

And she was. Sure, there'd been a few more paparazzi moments to remind her what she was getting into, but she was finding that she could get used to them and the attention—good and bad—of being with someone like Dylan. She could shut out all that noise for the most part, knowing that, in the end, she had Dylan and his love. That was all that mattered.

He was still trying to get her to move into his new place, the beautiful old Wallace place that she'd always wanted as her own—just like she'd always wanted the boy who lived there now. But for the time being, she was enjoying the courting they'd been doing, the late-night walks from his place back to the farm, where her dad was undoubtedly watching them from the front room window on those nights he wasn't out on his own date. It was probably also a good idea as they eased the brothers around the idea of the seriousness of their relationship. Tomorrow at Thanksgiving dinner would be a good test of that, and she grinned at the prospect.

"Why don't you take that to the truck and I'll be right there," she told him.

He stared at their faces again before giving her a quick wink. "Take your time."

They all watched him as he strutted out, and her stomach swirled at the fine specimen of a man he was and the fact that he was all hers.

Anna and Quinn laughed as they caught her face.

"What?" she asked defensively.

"Just that you look so deliriously happy," Quinn said.

"That and the fact you're practically a puddle on the floor of love—and a little lust," Anna added.

Tess snorted. "Like you could talk."

She stared at her friends. If she had to leave, she couldn't imagine a better time, what with all three entering the next stages of their lives with marriage just up ahead with men who loved them just as they deserved to be loved. "I guess this is it," she said a moment before they piled on her for one last hug.

When she joined Dylan in the truck and looked back at the two friends standing in the doorway a few minutes later, her heart was filled with love. Sadness, yes, but also a level of contentment. Whether they lived right down the hall from each other or an hour away or a thousand miles away, they would still have each other and their friendship.

She turned back to Dylan, her future. Even now, he still

could make her catch her breath, not just because he was easily the most handsome and sexiest man she'd ever known, but because of the way he could look at her with the same passion and love and excitement in his eyes. "I love you, you know."

He reached out and grabbed her hand, taking a second to touch it to his lips. "Not any more than I love you. Always and forever. You ready?" he asked, his eyes soft with emotion.

She took his hand and nodded. "For you? All my life."

Dylan finished stirring up the fire the next night and turned around to where Tessa was watching him from the couch. His heart thumped hard against his chest as he took a moment to just stare at the woman smiling back at him.

"Stop looking at me like that," she said and laughed.

"Like what?" he asked and crossed the short distance to sit next to her on the couch, taking a moment to slide her up against his side.

"You're looking at me like you did that giant pecan pie you had me make. Like you're going to devour me."

"Would that be such a bad thing?" he asked and leaned down to kiss her neck. He smiled as she shivered at his touch. He'd never get used to that.

"It would be if you pulled that in front of the boys," she said, meaning her brothers.

"Now, I think you sold them all short. They were practically cordial to me tonight at dinner," he bragged.

"Right, in between Finn pulling that chair out as you passed and Rowan accidentally spilling his ice water on your lap."

He grinned at the cheap plays, but he also knew that with the pranks there was also a growing acceptance that he was going to be in Tessa's life. If not, he'd likely have been mowed down by a tractor or poisoned by now.

"Why are you smiling?" she asked.

"No reason. But for all your nerves about having Thanksgiving together, I think things went pretty well."

She leaned her head against his shoulder and laced her hand into his. "It was wonderful. And I was relieved that Dad didn't bring any of the string of ladies he's been seeing with him tonight. That would have only made it awkward with Daphne."

He nodded. "Who knows, maybe one day he'll come around and see what was in front of him all along."

"I hope so, because I can't imagine anyone more fitting for him. Well, you know. Except for my mom."

He squeezed her hand. "I do. Your mom was a special lady. Hard to replace."

Dylan could say that now without feeling any of the usual loss and pain he had when he talked about moms. He'd come to terms finally with his past, accepted the weaknesses in the parents who'd both abandoned him in their own ways and forgiven them. He would choose to see all the positive things they'd offered him instead. Even his dad, who, the more he talked to Lana, he could see had never really stopped following Dylan's progress and had looked at him with pride. It all made him feel more complete.

Although nothing had come close to what having Tessa back in his life permanently had brought him. The joy and excitement for the future with her, whatever it might bring.

He looked up, knowing that someday this place would be filled with the running of little feet, with laughter and joy and many of their own holiday dinners and traditions.

Tessa was his family. His home. His life.

"You okay?" she asked softly, taking a moment to tuck a piece of hair back from his eyes, her touch, this simple showing of love, so welcome.

"Better than okay. Having you in my life? I'm truly blessed."

Coming soon...Crazy for the Royal!

Can't wait for the next book in the Crazy in Love Series?
Pick up my *USA Today* Bestseller Her Backup Boyfriend,
the first book in the Sorensen Family Series
HERE.

<<<<>>>>

ALSO BY ASHLEE MALLORY

Sweet Contemporary Romance

Crazy in Love Series:

Crazy for the Boss

Crazy for the Best Man

Crazy for the Rockstar

Crazy for the Royal (Coming Soon!)

Sorensen Family Series:

Her Backup Boyfriend

Her Accidental Husband

The Playboy's Proposal

Her Surprise Engagement

Romantic Suspense

You Again

Love You Madly

Thriller

Deceived

ABOUT THE AUTHOR

Ashlee Mallory is a *USA Today* Bestselling author of sweet romantic comedy, suspense, and thrillers. A recovering attorney, she currently resides in Utah with her husband and two kids. She aspires to one day include running, hiking, and traveling to exotic destinations in her list of things she enjoys, but currently settles for enjoying a good book and a glass of wine from the comfort of her couch.

Ashlee loves to hear from readers. You can find her at any of the following links, so please feel free to drop her a line, or subscribe to her email list and keep updated with any news of upcoming releases, sales, and giveaways by clicking here: Newsletter.

You can also find her on:

Facebook | Twitter | ashleemallory.com | Goodreads | Instagram